Murder
at the
Observatory

A Novel by

Christina Squire

Copyright ©2015 by Christina Squire

Cover concept by Charles Squire

Cover design by George Paloheimo Jr.

ABQ Press Trade Paper Edition 2015

www.abqpress.com

Albuquerque, New Mexico

ISBN 978-0-9916046-7-8

Acknowledgements

I could not have written this book without the advice and encouragement of my critique group. Heartfelt thanks to Lynn Miller and members of my writing group: Lynda Miller, Laurie Hause, Tina Carlson, Kim Feldman, and Jill Root.

I also thank Judith Van Gieson of ABQ Press for her patience and guidance through the publishing process.

I am grateful to my husband Bruce and our three sons for their love and support.

I have the deepest respect for the University of New Mexico Physics and Astronomy Department. I knew many brilliant and kind people during my years working there. Characters depicted in this mystery are dramatic creations and pure fiction.

ONE

This was the first September in my entire life that I had nothing to do. Until now I had always had three young children at home, taken classes at the university, and worked. After just a week I was ready to jump out of my skin and tear my hair out by the roots. I grabbed the want ads. Another long, jobless day loomed ahead. I was a hag without a future.

It started out a normal day. I woke up, stumbled into the kitchen, and poured a glass of orange juice for my son and me. Max, my 13-year-old "baby", was already up, showered, dressed, combed, and reading *The Albuquerque Journal* ads at the kitchen table. He forked cold, leftover spaghetti into his mouth with one hand and flipped pages with the other. I put his juice glass on the table. He was oblivious. I kissed the top of his head.

"Mom! Walgreens is having a special on batteries!" Ever since he could read, Max cut out coupons, and I paid him the money I "saved" at the store. He was a clever lad.

"Oh happy day," I mumbled as I poured some cream into the bottom of a coffee cup and zapped it in the microwave for twenty seconds. I filled my cup with coffee. Thank God my husband John made coffee before he went to work at his CPA firm. He was good for some things. I shook a can of Reddi-Wip. Max opened his mouth for a spray. My dog Suki ran in hearing the drizzly sounds. I sprayed cream in her mouth. I made a swirl on top of my coffee.

The spaghetti smell made me gag, so I went out to the backyard.

I walked to my vegetable garden. I talked to my tomato plants. I had read somewhere that one should talk to plants. OK. I was bored. I was thanking the vines for their bounty when the phone rang. Chatting! Verbal intercourse! With a human being! Maybe. I ran inside. Suki jumped around sharing my happiness.

It was Faye, my ex-supervisor at the Department of Physics and Astronomy. I knew it! She wanted me back!

"Caroline, I'm calling to tell you that Professor Cummings was discovered in the Observatory Saturday morning," she said without preamble.

"What was she doing? Tying up graduate students and beating them with her laser wand?"

Silence.

"No, she was quite dead."

"Oh my God!"

"I know she wasn't your favorite person in the world, but I thought you should know. The funeral will be Thursday at the Alumni Chapel."

"Will the Goddess of Astronomy be launched into space?"

Long silence.

I had better get serious. "Oh Faye! This is horrible! What do the police say? How did she die? Someone kill her?" I exclaimed in a higher pitched voice with a slight quiver. I was an actress whenever I could land a part.

"She was murdered. The police will hold a meeting with us. We'll hear the details then."

"Oh my. Let me know, OK?"

"You can find out yourself. The authorities want you here at noon tomorrow for briefing and questioning."

Silence.

"Why?" I asked with a real quiver in my voice.

"The officer had your name on a list."

"Why?" I asked again like an idiot.

"Someone in the department mentioned you specifically."

"Who?"

"Caro, I just know your name was on the list."

"Oh."

"I look forward to seeing you again. Sorry it's under these circumstances."

"Yeah…My sentiments exactly," I said.

Why did the police want to talk to me I wondered as I hung up the phone. My ears were ringing. I sat down at the kitchen table and looked at my handsome son as he microwaved a tortilla with cheese and green chili. Had he smoked a joint before breakfast? I didn't know anything anymore. And I did not know why I had to be questioned. I went back outside and collapsed in a lawn chair and leaned way back. I stared at the Sandia Mountains through my elevated feet. I watched my varicose veins drain.

Stella Cummings. What a piece of work she was. She terrorized staff and colleagues. I always felt that Stella was kept beyond her probationary period because she was willing to teach the huge Introduction to Astronomy classes with 300+ students and got excellent evaluations. She got voted outstanding teacher several years in a row. Also she published regularly thanks to her army of research assistants. She was a classic academic prize. And a bitch on wheels.

Max came out. He smelled of minty Crest and Sebastian Molding Mudd hair product. He kissed me good-bye. He still liked me. I said a little prayer of thanks that he was going to middle school instead of me. At mid-life I suffered a major identity crisis. I left my comfortable, convenient part-time secretarial job at the University of New Mexico two years ago to pursue a teaching certificate. I wanted to be "somebody". It took me all summer to recover from student teaching sixth graders last spring. My auburn hair was streaked with white and red veins exploded on my cheeks. I said shush a lot. I could not read or daydream. I applied with the Albuquerque Public Schools and had several interviews:

INTERVIEWER: "If I walked into your classroom, how would I know immediately that your students were learning?"

ME: "Well, they wouldn't be throwing rubbers across the room."

Alas, I had no offers. This school system has no sense of humor. I guess I could substitute teach. I would rather poke my eyes out with hot coals.

I made a bowl of Cheerios. I could not concentrate on the newspaper. Why oh why do the police want to interview me? I've been gone for two years. Someone must have said something. About Stella and me.

I emptied the dishwasher and began to load Max's pile and those from last night: ice cream bowls, wine glasses, nacho platters. I was getting fat.

At that thought I walked into the bedroom, dropped to my hands and knees and did ten cheater push-ups. I collapsed, rolled gracefully on my back, and flipped my legs up on the bed. Suki jumped up on the bed and hung her head over the side to get a good view. Crossing my arms artistically across my chest, I did 25 cheater sit-ups. Well, I was fit. Staring at the ceiling I thought about how someone must have told the authorities something. Probably that simpering Yvonne, the receptionist. There were no secrets in the Physics and Astronomy administrative office. The office manager, purchasing clerk, receptionist, student work-studies and I had all shared a large, open room surrounded by glass. It was like being in a zoo cage. Everyone heard and saw everything: certainly all my dealings with Stella. Certainly the phone call last month.

I sat up and leaned against the bed. Suki put her head on my shoulder. She knew something was wrong. I kissed her snout. I buried my head in her neck as I remembered the call from Stella.

We started out all fake friendly: How are you, I am fine, only to escalate into her screaming at me, and me telling her to fuck off.

"Will you tell your neighbor Brad that I need an article written in *The Albuquerque Journal*?"

"Well…" I started to answer.

"My latest discovery of the birth of new stars in the Orion Nebula has to be covered!"

"He's…" I said.

"He is not returning my calls or e-mails!"

"There's a reason for that! " I said.

"I know what you've done," Stella yelled. "You've poisoned his mind against me! You are just an underachieving woman jealous of successful women! I had you typed from the start!"

In truth, Brad, a managing editor at *The Journal*, had retired, but I didn't tell her that. I let her squirm. Brad was one of my trusted contacts in the local media. I had left the list with Stella. Very big of me, I thought at the time.

I knew she was calling from the main office when she crowed: "Fuck off? Caro just told me to fuck off everyone!" The diva always needed an audience.

I flushed thinking about Stella. My blood was boiling. Again.

I got up off the floor. I peeked into Douglas's room. My middle son had left for high school band practice at 6:30 this morning. His room was dark and smelled of 16-year-old male. I went to crack open a window, stubbed my toe on his futon, hopped around on one foot, and crashed into his drum set. I leaned against a wall to regain my balance next to a poster of nude men with teeny fur pelts covering their genitals. Rock and roll. I felt so old.

I got dressed. Took off my light weight hoody, plaid men's boxer shorts and black wife beater undershirt and put on Crocs, yoga pants, tissue tee. My darling look for home. I started my suzy housewife routine. I made the bed, changed Suki's water, topped off her food bowl, put out sun tea, emptied ice cube trays, picked up newspapers and magazines, straightened out the chaos in three bathrooms, put in a load of wash, and watered my plants.

I wandered into the den. Suki was now curled up on our $3,000 couch. I sighed. Wished I were a dog. I sat down at my computer. I wanted to write a novel that would make people laugh and cry. I stared. My mind was blank like the screen. Glancing around my desk for any inspiring scribbled notes, I spotted the newspaper article I was going to send to Peter, my first born, *Niño perfecto* son, who was a junior at the University of Texas at Austin majoring in advertising. The author described how advertisers are now catering to the baby boomer generation: more tartar control in our toothpaste and less Lycra in our clothes. I wrote a peppy note to include with the clipping, addressed and sealed the envelope and stuck it outside on the mail slot with a clothespin. I missed Peter so much. He was the sanest one in the family.

Now what? I picked up my knitting. I had been knitting a sweater monstrosity for John for over three years. I couldn't stop. I found a re-run of *The Avengers* on TV. I loved Emma Peele. She certainly could handle Lycra! I wished I looked like her. I knew she was having it off with Mr. Steed. My fantasies ran wild as I attacked the yarn. Knit, purl, knit, purl. Jab. Click. Oh Stella! Torturing me beyond the grave! I thought I was done with her. I flung the furry wad down. How dare the police want to talk to me?

My job had been public relations, writing press releases, promotional material: fliers, posters, newsletters, and catalogs. Stella tirelessly promoted the department. She perkily ran all over town speaking to groups and giving interviews on TV and radio. I scheduled them. Stella did not stand in front of my desk giving orders but walked around the desk and brayed into my face. She always invaded my personal space. Her long, wild, dry hair, ugly peasant skirts, porcine features, and scuffed Doc Martins offended me aesthetically. Her perfume burned my nostrils: Knowing by Estee Lauder. She left samples on my desk: "Try it! You'll like it!" I made a big show of throwing them away after she left. The staff watched

I will think about all this tomorrow! I will have an afternoon of peace. It was noon. The day goes. I made a sandwich, threw about 50 Tostitos on the plate, popped open a Diet Coke, and turned on the soap opera *General Hospital*. What trash but I couldn't stop watching it for the last 25 years. I hated all the characters and wished they would die in an explosion. I did the Jumble, Cryptoquip, and crossword puzzle so I didn't think I was wasting my time watching such drivel. After the soap opera was over, I cleaned up and did yoga. I felt good. Then I settled down on the couch with the dog to read *The Love Crescent*. A good friend had asked me to critique her Western Romance manuscript before she submitted it to be published. The sheer volume and weight hurt my neck trying to hold it up. My hands went to sleep. The love scenes were so hot. I kept imagining the author's sex life with her chemistry professor husband and getting jealous. Didn't you write what you knew? Well, shit. I could write a comedy about my sex life during tax season: CPA Husband Snores in His Finnish Orthopedic Chair While Wife Watches Colin Firth in *Pride and Prejudice* Jump in a Pond and Walk Out With Wet Shirt and Pants for the 50th Time Thus Causing Her to Reach a Crescendo In Her King Sized Bed Alone with Herself.

I rose off the couch and tore myself away from Jessie and Pilar, the main characters in *The Love Crescent*, who constantly had oral sex in whatever location they happened to be in. I welcomed my drummer Douglas when he came home from school. It was an emotional greeting. We grunted to each other. He went to the kitchen, made a chocolate shake, and ate cookies. I watched him fondly and thought about what to make for supper. John liked a big meal every night. I decided on pork chops. I flopped some in a shallow pan, dumped a jar of red chili on top, and put it in the oven with some potatoes. Dinner done.

Max walked in.

"How was your day, Mom?" he asked all smiles.

"Fine and dandy. Sweet as sugar candy," I replied as usual. "Where have you been?"

"At Jim's working on our science project. We're growing lima beans."

I looked at his pupils to see if they were dilated. We stared at each other close-up. He didn't flinch. I turned away first. I had forgotten to put my glasses on. I couldn't tell if he was (1) lying (2) stoned (3) both.

John came home. We had wine and a few ciggies out on our deck before dinner. This was our chummy routine. The boys left us alone. Peter and Douglas hated smoking. Max probably used this time to smoke out by the garbage cans. John and I usually gossiped and whined about our day. We were each good listeners, rather witty, we thought, and sympathetic, but I couldn't help but think it was all about me and he, of course, felt like it was all about him. We understood each other perfectly in this regard. And it was OK. And the wine helped. But when John launched into a verbal slash and burn on one of his business partners, I could only listen actively for so long. I blurted out: "Stella Cummings was found dead in the Observatory!"

"Who?"

"Stella Cummings! The Goddess of Astronomy! Her body was discovered early Saturday morning! She was probably killed Friday night. I don't know! The police want to talk to me tomorrow," I yelled. I wished he'd get a hearing aid.

"Oh her…do you need a lawyer?"

"I'm freaked, and you're joking."

"I'm not joking."

I looked into his hazel eyes. My mouth dropped open. He moved another lawn chair closer and put his legs up on it. He stretched his 6'4" body out. He lit a cigarette. "What?" He asked me all wide-eyed.

"You can't be serious!"

"Well, you did scream at her. Everyone heard. You told me. I'm just sayin'." He drained his glass. He got up. "More wine?"

I was near tears. "John! Don't make fun! I'm afraid I'm a suspect!"

John put his glass down. He took my hands and raised me up. He drew me into one of his bear hugs. I sobbed into his man boobs.

"Oh honey! You always go from A to C. This is not a catastrophe! You've let your imagination run away with you. Everything will be all right!" He lifted my tee and scratched my bare back. Heaven. He knew what I liked. I wrapped my arms around his ample waist. "I did not know you were so upset. I'm so sorry. I was kidding. I'm here for you. I love you, my sweet Caro."

"You know I'm not that sweet," I mumbled and wiped snot on his arm.

"So where were you Friday night?" he whispered in my ear.

I pushed him away. "Here watching *Pride and Prejudice!*"

"Are you sure?"

"Oh, shut up!" I spanked him.

John pulled me close. "I'll give you 45 minutes to cut that out." I stared at the tomato plants as his hand moved to my breast.

The next morning at 7 AM I found Max chewing on a cold pork chop. He reached the bone and sucked on it thoughtfully. He turned the newspaper pages with an elbow. I stared. Then I poured two glasses of orange juice.

"What would I do without my Mom?" Max said lovingly.

"Oh, honey." I said, so touched, and kissed the top of his shellacked head.

"Who would pour my orange juice?"

"Are you making fun of me?"

"Oh Mom!" He said as he jumped up and kissed me leaving a red chili smear on my cheek.

"Harrumph." I said as I made a bowl of Cheerios, but smiled. That child worked me.

What will I wear to the inquisition? Maybe a staid, teacher look: long plaid pleated skirt and crisp white blouse. I would make an artistic statement by accessorizing with griffin earrings.

I washed my hair in the kitchen sink. I loved my short hair. I towel dried it and spiked it up with Bed Head Manipulator. Steven, my stylist, did a great job. Stella hated my hair.

I applied eyeliner with shaking hands remembering the outburst with Stella that will probably do me in. I blew powder off my eye-shadow brush. Show time.

TWO

I pulled into the parking lot behind the Physics and Astronomy building. I walked purposefully through the double doors into the lounge area filled with ugly Naugahyde sofas and chairs. The colorful, dramatic astronomy posters I had ordered from planetariums around the country still hung on the walls. I suddenly realized how much I missed this place. It was the first job I had after all three boys were in school. The professors were by and large friendly, if distant. They were doing God's work after all.

I saw the office staff gathered in the glass enclosed main office. They were unusually quiet. Yvonne came up to me first and gave me a big hug. What a sweet, ambitious receptionist.

"I was so glad you told Stella to fuck off," she whispered in my ear. I knew it, I thought!

Still being held in a vice grip, I looked over her big hair at Lorraine, our purchasing clerk. Actually I could only see her nose, inner corners of her eyes, and the middle of her lips. Shoulder length dyed blonde hair, parted down the middle, hid most of her face.

"How are you, Caro?" Lorraine was a woman of few words

and penetrating stares. She spoke through clenched teeth. Her uniform was black skirts, white blouses, and black heels.

"Hi, Caro." I disentangled myself from Yvonne's smothering embrace to shake Hal's extended hand. Poor old dense Hal: Administrative Assistant to the Chairman. But what a build! All his blood never got to his brain. Hal worked out every noon hour and rode his bike to work from the west side of town. He was so kind and incompetent. After a series of anxiety-ridden, hysterical women in this difficult position, Hal was like an angel of mercy for the Chair of the Department.

"I am s-sorry you had to come b-back under these circumstances. How are your boys?" Dolores, the accountant, stammered in a high-pitched voice. Pale, thin, with long, shoulder-length gray hair and wearing the same gray polyester pant and faded leopard print shirt combination she's worn for years. She just stood next to me looking concerned. She wasn't into physical contact. Dolores didn't drive, lived with her demented mother, and read pussycat mysteries. She only ate at McDonald's.

I felt a soft touch on my arm. I turned to Faye, Office Manager, mediator of bitches, faculty soother, dog rescuer, organizer of lives, tiny, cute…mother. Her reddish blonde hair was cut in a short bob with aggressively permed teeny waves radiating out from the razor sharp side part. One side of crinkly curls was pulled back tightly in a colorful barrette. She had a different one for every day of the month. Today's choice had purple feathers that matched her purple jumper and purple socks. On her dainty feet were black flats with black bows. Faye smelled of a heady blend of Youth Dew perfume and cigarettes. Chewed nails were polished pink. She had a backbone of steel.

Faye put her arm around my waist. Her blue eyes radiated concern.

"The police are here to question us," she said, patted me on the back, and led us all down to the smoking lounge where no one can smoke anymore.

THREE

As I walked down the long hallway, I passed a few faculty members shuffling by with their heads down. All of them needed decent clothing, shampoos, and matching socks. They are too busy for such time wasters thinking about the universe, novas, supernovas, worm holes, black holes, dark matter, hyperspace, strings, and fractals. Each professor hopes they will be the one to discover the answer to the big question: What is exactly going on out there? We passed one of the two displays I designed. The glass awards cabinet had portraits of the department's finest. There was Henry (Hank) Burns the world expert on swiss-cheese holes in space. I got off on the wrong foot with him when I wrote a press release calling him Dr. Frank Burns. ("How dare you associate me with the worst character on MASH?") He was pompous, but I made a very bad mistake. We never got along after that. He never got along with Stella Cummings, either.

As we turned down another hall, I looked at the photo gallery of current graduate students. I had such fun taking Polaroid pictures of them when they arrived from all over the world. I did care for the young people here---especially those Greek guys.

"Chica!" I turned around to see the custodian, Griselda, coming down the hall with a push broom. I ran to her, bent over and buried my head in her crisp uniform. She held me tight while swaying back and forth whispering *mi hija* over and over again. She always smelled so good: Not a hair out of place, full make-up, polished nails, wearing high top red Converse tennis shoes. Griselda was from Colombia. I loved her.

She leaned back and started laughing. Her silver capped teeth flashed.

"Oh Chica! I have missed you!"

"I've missed you, too!"

Griselda stood on her tiptoes and kissed me on the cheek. I started to cry. All the stress of the past welled up in me. I spent a year in abject grief over the loss of my brother then threw myself into wretched education classes; student teaching for a year under a psycho babe cooperating teacher. I had worked so hard to get my certificate and now didn't want to teach. My children were becoming strangers. I was in a marriage rut. Griselda's outpouring of affection reached the deepest, most vulnerable part of me that I had kept locked in order to get through my days.

She handed me a perfectly ironed snowy white handkerchief from her apron pocket. I wiped my eyes and nose.

"Hey! You crying over our favorite queen of astronomy? May she roast in Hell! Si? No? Hey! Chica! Answer me!"

I started laughing. "I have to go to a meeting." I handed back her hankie.

"Keep it, Chica, and *vaya con Dios!*"

FOUR

We filed into the lounge and sat on more unattractive, cracked Naugahyde couches. A tall, distinguished-looking man dressed in a tweed sports jacket and beige chinos looked out the window. He turned around and walked to the center of the room. All of us squirmed except Faye.

"Hello. My name is Inspector James Hutchinson. I work in the Albuquerque Police Department Homicide Division. I am here to get a general impression from each of you on Dr. Cummings state of mind during the week before her death, and if anything out of the ordinary happened."

He took a notebook out of his jacket pocket. James had beautiful green eyes.

"As you know, Dr. Stella Cummings was found Monday morning in the Observatory at 7:00 AM by a plumber from the Physical Plant. She was in the Green Room. The cause of death was suffocation. There was no sign of a struggle. The time of death has been determined to be between midnight and 2:00 AM Saturday morning."

"She was the faculty advisor on duty for public night," Faye said, "John Brooks and Katie Chu were the graduate students assisting her."

"I have spoken to them," Mr. Hutchinson said. "Dr. Cummings told them to leave before the observatory closed at 10:00, and she would lock up. They went straight to O'Neill's Pub to meet friends and stayed until closing. Now who would like to comment first on any unusual behavior concerning Dr. Cummings last week?"

Yvonne piped up: "She had an abnormal amount of calls from a radio station. She was supposed to go on the air last Thursday to talk about a new planet, or something, and to promote the Observatory Open Night. She left orders for us in the office that she was not accepting calls all week because of female problems so her phone was automatically transferred to the front office. She said she could barely teach her 101 classes. She looked pale and nervous. Have you checked her office for the hundreds of messages I took?"

Oh the same old same old, I thought to myself, as I tore my eyes away from the handsome detective to the small chip in the window behind him. In happier times, the office staff would drink cokes, smoke, and laugh with graduate students here on breaks. One young post-doc in physics demonstrated the density X velocity strength of a Moon Pie by throwing it at the window. The window cracked. The Moon Pie did not even dent.

"We searched her office and found no messages dated from last week."

"Well, we certainly took enough!" Lorraine said dryly. "We have always been her personal secretaries. It's not our job! We take calls if she has a hangnail. I've had to schedule house painters and veterinarian appointments for her cat."

Oh God, I'm glad I'm out of here. Give me 6th graders any day. At least they're funny.

"So she suffered from PMS?" Mr. Hutchinson asked.

Lorraine rolled her eyes.

Faye said gently, " Why don't you tell him what happened last week."

Lorraine exploded. "This was NOT in my job description! I got a call on my personal line: 'Help me. Help me.' I knew it was Stella's voice. I asked what was wrong. She asked me to come to her office. When I opened her door, she was standing up with blood running down her legs. She cried 'help me' again. I told her I would get some paper towels. And I did. And I left. End of story."

"Was she under a doctor's care?" asked the detective.

"She saw doctors for everything: her back, her uterus, her feet, her eyes," Faye replied.

"Chocolate helped her during her menstrual time," Yvonne added.

Poor Stella needed love. Too bad, so sad, I thought, while I admired James's beautiful hands. I felt two eyes boring into me. Faye. She was picking up my negative waves. She was uncanny that way.

Hal finally came down to earth: "She was very angry Friday afternoon. She was furious that she had to be the faculty advisor at the observatory. She yelled at me, and said that she did enough to promote this department. I told her that the schedule was drawn up and approved by all the astronomers, including her, before fall semester started. Then she screamed about how this macho oriented department took advantage of her. We hired her only to use her and suck her dry. She was sick and tired of all men." Hal shook his head and then smiled. Very odd. Maybe he was thinking of his bicycle. You never knew.

"I-I got a call from NASA concerning the grant proposal she submitted last spring," Dolores said. "They would not be able to come up with the funds she requested. Due to b-budget cuts, NASA has discontinued some of their star research. She almost s-stroked out when I gave her the news. She lashed out at me and twirled around my office like a whirling dervish. She screamed for me to get money for her! That she needed the g-grant to apply for a position at the Alma Radio Telescope in Chile. I screamed back at her that I was an accountant n-not a magician. Geesh."

Poor Dolores. Poor office staff. These were not isolated incidents. Stella acted out constantly. Her behavior last week was business as usual. I started to entertain myself (again) with vicious thoughts about the dead.

Silence in the lounge grew. I hadn't said anything. Why was I really here? All of us were fidgeting…except Faye.

Mr. Hutchinson finally spoke: "So If I may summarize what is known about the week before Stella's death. She suffered from PMS, was disappointed that her grant was denied, failed to show up for a radio program, and felt unfairly treated by the department. Stella was argumentative and combative."

We all stared at him.

"Please write a statement of where you were Friday night. I'll pick them up tomorrow. Now I want to speak to Faye and Mrs. Steele alone. The rest of you can go. Thank you for your time. I may have more questions for you later."

My mouth went dry. Yvonne crushed me into her ruffled blouse and whispered "Good luck." Faye closed the door after everyone left. Now I really was afraid.

FIVE

"We found something of yours in Stella's office," Mr. Hutchinson looked at me and reached into his pocket. He pulled out a small object and held it up to me. There was my notebook with a picture of a smiling woman wearing an apron in front of an open door of a full refrigerator. The caption Make Your Own Damn Dinner was scrawled over it.

"I wondered where that was!" I exclaimed. "I must have left it in my desk drawer. How did Stella get it?"

"I don't know," the Inspector said, "but there are some pretty negative writings about Stella in here."

I felt all the blood rushing to my head. I was hot. My ears started to ring. I started to babble:

"I am an anxious scribbler. You probably read all my notes taken at Sunday school! My trips to Seattle and New York! My impressions of my sons' girlfriends! And all the books I want to read. And my inspirational quotes, mattress recommendations...." I started to fade out, but rallied. "It isn't all about Stella."

"No, you're right," he said as he flipped through the pages. "What an observant person you are; most entertaining reading. Reminds me of Cecily's line in *The Importance of Being Earnest*: 'I never travel without my diary. One must always have something sensational to read on the train.'"

"Thank you." I guess he gave me a compliment. I didn't mind my writing being called sensational. And James quoted Oscar Wilde. Fascinating. The inspector was rather sensational. I quit my imaginings as he read:

"Got my haircut at Steven's Family Hair Care. I really like his thighs. Stella hates my short hair. She whispered in my ear that I looked like a man. I hate that bitch. Fuck her."

"So Stella thought you looked like a man?" he asked as he scribbled in his notebook. The corners of his mouth twitched.

Faye reached over to pat my hand. "Oh, Caro. I'm so sorry. Everyone has whiskers and things."

My hand automatically covered my mustache. I had not waxed since I was jobless.

"Here's another one: Stella left a sample of Knowing on my desk. I didn't touch it. She sailed through the office and asked why I hadn't opened it. Like I want to smell like a whorehouse? Not. She said that I should wear scent. Do I have BO? She's crazy and irritates the shit out of me."

I sighed. Faye patted my hand again.

"There was a bottle of Knowing perfume next to the Godiva chocolates in the Observatory," James said.

I looked at Faye. She was idly brushing imaginary crumbs off the couch.

He continued: "She asked me why I dressed like my teenage daughter. I told her I didn't have a teenage daughter. Excuse me if I'm not a fashion don't. Stella needs a black bar over her eyes. Ugly aging woman in hippie clothes: Beady eyes, witchy hair, piggy nose, pendulous tits. She needs a boob reduction. Hell, she needs massive work done in Guadalajara, Mexico."

"Do I need a lawyer?" I asked.

"You have to understand, Inspector," Faye rushed in. "Caro dealt with Stella from the first day she arrived. She made her feel welcome. In fact, she was the nicest person to her. We still miss Caro!" More pats.

"So you two used to get along?"

I swallowed, but my throat was so dry that I croaked, "We would chat about children. She lost custody of her son. She had wretched parents. I felt so sorry for her. She loved astronomy--the wonder of it all and so did I--as a mystical as well as a scientific discipline. I was taking Astronomy 101 at the time from another instructor. I had to learn some astronomy basics to answer the phone calls from people who had questions. Like: I saw something in the sky. What was it?"

I hoped to get a laugh. Dead air.

"Caro dealt with the public. You were so polite to all the weirdos and crack-pots," Faye said gently.

I looked at Faye and squeezed her hand hard. She stopped patting me.

"I missed a class, and Stella invited me to make it up with her. She was so dynamic on that stage. She never lectured but expounded on the drama of the universe like lines from a classic play. She said space was not dark but filled with light and color. She kept moving as she talked, long hair whipping around, stopping only to look up at a magnificent slide of an object in space. Her face would be in ecstasy. As an actress, I was very impressed by her performance. Such energy and projection! I admired her!"

"Even though she harassed you."

"That started about a year later. I stopped speaking to her. Then I left to get my teaching certificate."

"Why did she start to harass you?"

"She wanted me to book all of her public appearances. I had contacts with the media and thought I would help her get started in town since she was new. Professors usually schedule their own speaking engagements. My job was to write press releases, but…."

"But?"

"She wouldn't like the venue, she wasn't treated well, she alienated many of my contacts, and this reflected on me. They called me to ask why I just didn't come and talk about upcoming events. Who was this prima donna? I wished I could have." I glanced at Faye but she was adjusting her barrette. "She accused me of sabotaging her public image by placing her in inferior programs with idiotic announcers at bad times. I would never do that. She sabotaged herself."

"Caro mentioned some of her concerns to me," Faye said, hair now securely constrained. "I counseled her to stop making Stella's public appointments and ignore her. I mentioned to the chair how rude Stella was to the staff. He was in a tight spot academically. Stella published regularly and her classes got excellent evaluations. He told me to deal with office matters."

"Looks like you were documenting to bring a grievance," James said looking at me.

"I wouldn't take the energy over someone like her. I just wanted to go on to something else."

"But not before you 'had it out with her'?"

"I went to her office and told her to leave me alone. That's all."

"That's all?"

"Yes."

"And did she?"

"Kinda sorta."

"Caro was going through personal grief, too. Her brother was killed in a car accident," Faye said.

"Stella would have pissed me off anyway."

"Caro took only three days off. She is so strong,"

"Not really," I answered. I felt myself tearing up. I did not want to talk about my brother and Stella in the same breath. Now that was a crime.

"I'm sorry for your loss," the detective said.

"Thank you."

"I'm keeping this notebook as evidence."

"Whatever. It's just my feelings in that particular time and space. It's so sophomoric! I'm embarrassed! I've moved on. And Stella's gone."

"Indeed. Where were you Friday night?"

"I was home watching *Pride and Prejudice* with my husband."

"The Colin Firth *Pride and Prejudice*?

"Of course."

"Of course." Mr. Hutchinson scribbled in his pad. "Did you have any contact with Stella after you left Physics and Astronomy?"

"God no."

"That will be all for now. Thank you for your time. I will contact you all in the future with updates. I wish you both a very good day."

Faye and I stood up. James shook our hands. His was warm. Mine was clammy. He left. I looked at Faye. Her blue eyes were slits staring at a wall. I tried to break the tension.

"I feel like *Harriet the Spy* when someone discovered her diary."

Faye started to fumble through her purse.

"Have you read *Harriet the Spy*?" No reply. Faye dug through the bottom of her bag frantically. I rattled on: "She kept a diary and wrote smack about fellow school mates. Someone found the diary and exposed her. She had to apologize and eat humble pie, so to speak. I can't do that, obviously."

"That fucking bitch," Faye said between clenched teeth and lit a cigarette under the No Smoking sign. I joined her. "Stella has been a thorn in my side for years. She blocked my office chi."

I patted her hand.

SIX

"I just don't know."

"What?"

"I just don't know."

"Don't know what?

"What to think!"

"Stop thinking. And get away from that magnifying mirror. You spend hours in front of it like you're in a crack den."

"I have to pluck this hair growing out of my chin. It's stiff and white."

"Jesus. No one can see it."

My husband and I were getting ready for bed. John was rubbing colloidal oatmeal cream on his hands and feet.

"Please pass the unguent."

I put down my tweezers and gave him the La Natura Vanilla Lip Balm. I squirted Ocean up my nose, rubbed Vicks under my nostrils, and slathered on lavender foot cream. John passed me the cuticle cream after he was done. I turned off the light, and we slithered under the sheets. A medley of smells hung like a cloud over our football field sized bed.

"I think I'm a suspect."

"You're paranoid. And you're bored. You get weird when you have nothing to do. You need a job."

"What I need is something to wear to the funeral tomorrow."

"Jesus. What a glutton for punishment. Give us a kiss."

SEVEN

The day dawned. I stared into my closet filled with ugly teacher clothes. No wonder most women (and men) look so tacky in front of a public school classroom. Who has time to shop after a week of torture and a weekend of grading and planning? Maybe I should wear all white. Episcopal funerals are resurrection services. No, I would look too happy, pure, and cleansed. I will not wear all black. Too sad. I settled on a mixture of feelings with a white long skirt and black tee. Only Dansko clunkers and athletic shoes lined the bottom of my closet. Horrible.

The university was still in session so I knew the parking around the Alumni Chapel would be full. I parked by my church several blocks away and walked through the old adobe neighborhood to the campus. What a lovely day. I had to adjust my smiling face but not yet. I passed by the Student Union Building, Zimmerman Library, and on by the Duck Pond. Couples lay out on the lush grass in each other's arms kissing and whispering head to head. Ah life, love, and the pursuit of happiness. I missed passion. John and I had our moments, but we were tired, or something. My body needed some pulsing, throbbing, thrusting, explosive....

"Hello, Mrs. Steele," Detective Hutchinson fell into step with me. I looked into his Ray-Bans. I got hot all over. My ears started ringing. I fell off my clog. He grabbed my arm and yanked me up as I went down.

"Oh thank you. I am such a dork," I said as I tried to put my shoe back on while teetering on one leg. He didn't let go of me.

"Don't be silly. Happens to me all the time."

"You fall off your clog?"

"Well, yes."

"Dansko's?"

"Of course."

He was wearing a black pinstriped suit with an aquamarine shirt and teal tie. He smelled like an ocean breeze. I just stared at him. After what seemed like an hour, he dropped my arm, unfortunately, and made an "after you" gesture.

"Shall we go?"

"We shall." We walked silently by Scholes Hall and the Anthropology Museum.

"This is a beautiful campus," he said.

"Thank you," I said stupidly. He looked at me. I regained my wits. "Yes, isn't it! You haven't been here before?"

"No"

"Are you new to Albuquerque?"

"I just moved here from New Orleans."

"I had one of the best times of my life there. I felt like I was in another country."

"The city has its charms."

"Welcome to Albuquerque!"

"Thank you."

Silence.

"So where did you park?"

"I took the bus."

"What? I bet you made a lot of new best friends wearing that suit."

"The bus has its charms."

I was dying here. "So you are going to Stella's funeral." He nodded his handsome head. "Looking for the murderer?" Silence. "I've read enough mysteries to know that the killer often attends the funeral of the victim." Silence. "Ha ha," I rattled on, "Novels! I read too much!"

"Not possible," he said. He stood still, removed his sunglasses and looked at me. His green eyes complimented his shirt, tie, and entire body.

"My sentiments exactly," I whispered.

He lightly touched my elbow as we walked into the Alumni Chapel. James nodded at me then turned to talk to a man in a university police uniform. I just stood there. What was going on? Were they expecting a riot? Out of control swooning? Hundreds of illegally parked cars? Someone going postal? ("My favorite teacher is dead! I gave her an excellent evaluation! My life in Astronomy is over! I Die! And so will you!") I felt a thin arm like vise go around my waist.

"Oh Caro. I knew you would come," Faye said softly. Today her barrette was a crescent moon on cloud of black lace.

"You told me to," I said distractedly as I watched James over her curls. She led me down the aisle. I breathed in the coolness of the whitewashed, thick adobe walls, the wood beams in the ceiling, the hand carved pews. I loved this chapel. So spare and clean. I looked at the bare altar and gasped. There was a casket. It was open. I grabbed Faye's hand. Memories of all the Macedonian funerals I had attended came to me. I felt light headed. My mother's side of the family grieved loudly and physically. People would try to climb into the casket crying, "Let me go with you." Mourners lifted up corpses and kissed them. The bodies were laid out for days: So much screaming and wailing. Surely this would not happen here. I never looked at my brother's body. I could not. I could not.

I breathed deeply. I will not look inside the casket. I felt better. I sat down. I let Faye's hand go. She put her arm around me. I looked past her and saw the rest of the office staff. Hal had his eyes closed. Dolores was working a crossword puzzle. Lorraine was staring straight ahead. Yvonne was folding and unfolding a handkerchief. I saw the faculty sitting across the aisle. Most of them are such sweet men. They even combed their hair. The astronomers were in one pew silently looking at the ceiling. They were used to looking up. The chair of the Department, Astronomer Brad Winter, was whispering into his smart phone. I noticed a very healthy head of shiny, jet black hair. So Hank Burns drove up from New Mexico State. Interesting. He was examining his nails.

The physicists were in another pew with heads down. Some were dozing, and some were writing on the service bulletin. They passed the programs back and forth either nodding in agreement or scribbling additions. I had witnessed this behavior over the years. Mostly they wrote on the donut napkins during colloquiums. It was like they thought of something and had to write it down immediately: formulas, theories, fractals, etc. Always thinking those guys.

All the faculty sat dry-eyed.

I twisted around to look for my inspector. Griselda was sitting in the back row wearing her custodial uniform and a long black veil.

I heard sobbing. I turned back around to see Faye leaning forward to whisper in a woman's ear who was sitting in front of us. She looked at Faye and mouthed "thank you." It was sweet Cecilia DeBlasi sniveling into an embroidered handkerchief. This was the same graduate student who told me that Stella made her life hell on earth? I was confused. Where was the blue bandana that covered her head at all times? Luxurious strawberry blonde curls flowed down to her shoulders and hung over the back of the pew. Wow. Faye sat back. I turned to her to say something, but she elbowed me and mouthed the word 'don't'.

An older couple walked down the aisle with an obese young man and sat in the front pew. This must be Stella's son. He looked to be in his late teens. And those were the loving parents. Stella told me what they said to her:

"You've made our life miserable. We wish you would have died instead of your brother."

Well, no wonder Stella was so screwed up and determined to succeed. She showed mommy and daddy dearest. I actually started to feel sorry for her.

The pale, spotty son sat hunched between his grandparents. Stella lost custody of him when she was eighteen and wanted to go to college. Her father sued for custody because he said a two year old needed a mother figure at home at all times. Grandma gave up her bridge clubs and charity work until the boy was in the first grade. Stella told me this while tears glistened in her eyes. She only got to see Brian for two weeks during the summer, she said, but I wondered. She never brought him to work. Sad stories, but she had screaming conversations about money with the boy on the front office phones. The drama queen did not have an audience in her own office.

A thin young man in jeans and a polo shirt walked up in front of the casket. He started the service by reading passages from *Cosmos* by Carl Sagan then continued on with his homily: We are but stardust. In death we will join the trillions and trillions of stars to shine upon the earth. We will return to the universe to regenerate in a supernova of love. In life we are as grains of sand. His talk was sincere, but he sounded like he was from the Universal Church of What's Happening Now.

Suddenly Cecilia DeBlasi leapt up. She was not wearing her usual denim overalls, plaid shirt, and Red Wing boots. She was poured into a thigh-high red dress with a plunging neckline. Black fish net hose covered shapely long legs. Black stiletto heels did not slow her down as she raced to the front of the chapel. Wow. What an entrance! She yelled: "I have to sing a song for Stella!" The preacher jumped back. In a shaky falsetto she started Joni Mitchell's *Woodstock* building to an ear splitting crescendo when she got to the last verse about humans being stardust and the devil catching them in his bargain so they had to get free and get back to the garden, and so forth and so on.

Someone applauded. Cecilia looked at the congregation with wild eyes. She exclaimed, "Stella was caught in the devil's bargain at the Department of Physics and Astronomy! They mistreated and maligned a woman of great talent. But you devils know the bargain you made! You loved her class numbers, her evaluations, her research, her drive! You drove a hard bargain for a true scholar! You made her miserable and sucked her dry!" She pointed a shaky finger at the faculty. "You devils know who you are! An exceptional woman is dead. Dead! Now she is in the garden of heav--"

The young minister sprinted up to Cecilia and put his arm around her. "Thank you so much for sharing. We feel your pain. God bless you." He tried to steer her toward the aisle. Cecilia shrugged him off, burst into tears, and rushed to Stella's family to hug each of them. They sat stiffly during this display of emotion. Cecilia ran back to her seat and covered her face with the pretty hankie. Hank Burns got up and walked out of the chapel. His fellow astronomers squirmed. The Chair put his phone in his shirt pocket. The physicists kept comparing notes and seemed oblivious. (Did they ever notice anything in the real world?) I tried to get Faye's attention, but she ignored me. Instead she reached over, stroked Cecilia's bowed head, and gave me another jab with her elbow. "Ow," I said. Faye stroked my head.

"Thank you very much, Miss…er…ah…yes, thank you, lovely, honest, honestly lovely for sure," the flustered cleric said. "Anyone else like to say or sing anything about Stella?"

"I do!" All heads turned to see Michael O'Dowd coming down the center aisle. He winked at me as he went by. His wild red hair was sticking out at all angles. He wore huge coke-bottle thick glasses. His baggy jeans hung down his butt, and he wore a green Rock'n Bowl shirt with a huge bowling ball on the back. Instead of just walking in his tattered black Converse tennis shoes, he lurched and shuffled with an odd rhythmic pattern. (He covered a lot of ground with one lurch and two shuffles.) A genius in Thermodynamics, Michael was one of the most eccentric Physics professors in the department. And that was saying something. I liked his act.

He stood next to Stella's coffin and held on to the side. He boomed:

"Well, wasn't she a little spitfire? I'll say! She showed up all of us guys! Her classes huge! Her evaluations grand! Her goals worthy! Her determination legion! Snuffed out at the apogee of her career. Ah so sad. But Stella accomplished so much in her short time strutting on earth. May she be kicking academic ass on another planet as I speak. God bless her! And God bless us everyone…her most humbled colleagues."

Michael patted the coffin and put his hand to his heart over his embroidered name. Then he lurched/shuffled back down the aisle.

Silence. The minister trotted up to the front.

"Ok, so peace be with you and have a good day." He bolted out the side door.

Thank God this was over, I thought. But no. Stella's parents and son started walking up to the casket. Every aisle emptied out and followed them.

"We have to go up and offer our condolences," Faye said as she herded me toward the front of the chapel.

"I think I'll pass. They don't know me. I don't want to," I protested.

"Come on," Faye hissed.

We stood in line. I looked everywhere but the casket. I thought about James. I stared at my clogs, God bless them. I squinted my eyes like I did at scary movies. I looked over Faye's head and saw Stella's son stop in front of the casket fumbling with a small tin can. He opened it and poured the contents over his mother's body. Now I HAD to look in the casket. I was shocked. There was Stella's round, pasty dead face surrounded by spikey short hair. Her long hair, her crowning glory, was gone! And she was dotted with what looked like dark pebbles.

"When did she cut her hair?" I whispered to Faye after shaking the limp hands of the family and making sympathetic noises. "Did you see the black doodads?"

"Shh," she hissed.

I was in a daze. I could not get outside fast enough. I walked into the shade of a cottonwood tree. I saw my inspector sitting on a bench talking on the phone. I marched (carefully) over to him. He had a bemused expression on his face as he rang off. I wished he'd take off those damn sunglasses.

"See anybody suspicious?" I asked.

"I will not say."

"Well, I saw something suspicious! The son dropped tiny balls on his mom, and Stella's hair is chopped off."

"I know."

"You know what?"

"I know her hair was short."

"And the little round stuff?

"Well, no, but thanks for telling me. I'll make note."

"That's nice. So you knew about her hair?"

"Yes."

"Stella hated short hair! Did you know that?"

"Yes."

"How could you know how Stella felt about hair?"

"I am an inspector. I inspect."

"Then why didn't you mention this in the interview?"

"I wanted to see your reaction."

"Oh, did you now? So you saw, Mr. Hutchinson. And now I have to go do something. Good-bye." I turned slowly, and I hoped gracefully, around.

"Just a minute, please," he said. I had a minute, I thought, and turned back. He took my ratty notebook out of his pocket, flipped through some pages, stopped and read. "Do you still go to Steven's Family Hair Care?"

"I do. Why are you still carrying around my notes? Don't those belong on a shelf in an evidence room behind an iron gate under lock and key?"

"They are safe in my pocket."

"I'm sure," I said and then snapped out of my imaginings. "Did Steven cut Stella's hair?"

"I don't know. There's a red star by his name and number." He held up the page to me. "Did you draw that?"

"No! I never use red ink."

"Thank you for your time, Mrs. Steele," James said as he tucked my notebook back into his pocket.

Once again I found myself speechless and unable to move until I heard Faye call my name.

EIGHT

Faye suggested the staff eat Greek for lunch at the Olympia Café.

"What? No reception?" I asked.

"No one planned anything," Faye murmured. "Sad."

We walked over to Central Avenue. I loved the old part of this campus: The tree-lined pathways, the soft curves of the adobe structures, the recessed, large windows, and the way the sun cast rounded shadows off the buildings. I looked fondly at Scholes Hall. My first job after high school was working 20 hours a week in the cashier's office while taking a full load of classes. For the first time I was around divorced women. They laughed a lot. What a rowdy group. I learned to use a calculator and smoke.

I wanted to talk about the funeral, but everyone was subdued. We crossed at the light at Yale on Central Avenue, the old Route 66, and longest road in the US. One would think the 60s were alive and well with decrepit characters shuffling around begging, walking mangy dogs and goats, guitars strapped on backs, long greasy hair, heavy smells of pot and incense, homeless selling homeless news, and Rastafarians in street dividers playing bongos and singing. I saw my favorite character on Central: a person dressed like a Mexican wrestler wearing a signboard for Bandito Hideout. He stood on a street divider pointing at the restaurant wearing red shiny tights, black patent leather boots, a long sleeved leotard with neon green and yellow lightning bolts, a red cape, and a silver mask that covered his face with sinister black slits for his eyes, nose, and mouth. I did so enjoy Central Avenue. I lived close to Central further east, but we just had hookers parading up and down drinking Big Gulps.

We stood in line at Olympia to place our order. "What? No hamburgers? Sh-shoot!" Dolores exclaimed when she read the menu on the wall. She left. The head cook slammed prepared food on the counter, read the order slip, and screamed out a name. The person rushed up for his tray. They better not be late or the cook would scream again. I was reminded of my Macedonian family. They were always screaming even if you were standing right in front of them. I felt rather warm and fuzzy. I could not talk with this commotion, so I stood silently like everyone else until I chose a gyros and glass of wine. I needed it. We picked up our drinks and walked into the seating area.

Faye picked a long table in the back of the restaurant. I sat down next to her fairly bursting with my observations. Being a lookist at heart, I had to talk about Sweet Cecilia.

"So she does have breasts!" I exclaimed.

"I'll say," Hal said and took a swig of his beer.

"But are they real?" Yvonne asked primly as she sipped lemon water.

"And what was with that dress? I think it's bizarre that Cecilia morphed into a dancer from the Kit Kat Club," I said.

"Maybe she's free now to explore being a girl," Hal offered.

"Who or what prevented her before?" Lorraine asked.

"She had an image to maintain," said Hal.

"She hid her beauty! Why?" I was all excited with possibilities. I started to answer my own question, but Faye cut me off.

"Oh please!" Faye said as she squeezed lime into her Diet Coke. "Someone killed Stella. Let's not talk about Cecilia's breasts or clothes."

"Excuse me if I am more interested in Cecilia than Stella!" I protested. "And there could be some connection! Her outburst was totally shocking! Stella ruined her chances of applying for medical school last year by delaying her thesis evaluation. And when it came, it was negative! So why did she defend her?"

Faye said dryly, "Cecilia can always join her sister on stage."

"What?" We all said in unison.

Dolores walked up to the table with a bag of McDonald's drinking a miniscule Senior Coke. She plopped down. "What did I m-miss?"

We started talking at once but were drowned out when the chef yelled out our names one after the other. Music to my ears!

"I want to know about Stella's hair. Did any of you know she was getting it cut?" Faye asked as she sliced off a dainty piece of Greek chicken.

Everyone shook their heads.

I said, "James, er, Inspector Hutchinson, showed me my notebook where Stella had starred Steven's Family Hair Care's phone number," I confided quietly to Faye.

"Well, he'll certainly contact him. The graduate students working at the Observatory that night can tell us if her hair was cut that night. The murderer may have hacked it off."

"Didn't look like a hack job to me. I thought it was rather cute and artistic. Gave her some cheekbones."

"Oh Caro."

"Too late for style, poor thing," I sighed taking a huge bite of gyros dripping taziki sauce down my shirt.

"W-where did Hank Burns run off to?" Dolores mumbled through a mouth full of hamburger.

"Maybe he had to make a phone call. To Chile," Lorraine deadpanned. She slid a piece of pork souvlaki off a skewer with her tiny, sharp teeth.

"He had to have known that Cecilia was talking to him," Faye said as she peeled all the skin off her chicken.

"But he's been gone for over a year," I said. "What about Chile?"

"B-Burns and Stella had submitted proposals to use the new Alma Observatory in Chile," Dolores answered.

Hal emptied his beer bottle. He picked up the entire half chicken with his hands. He tore off a chunk. He waved a joint dripping with juice and tendons as he added, "They only take a few people a year from each of the countries that financed Alma. There are major competitions going on in Europe, East Asia, North America and, of course, Chile. Stella and Burns were the only astronomers in the southwest United States applying." That said, he took an enormous bite of meat, smiled, and chewed with his mouth open. He looked at us all so satisfied with himself.

Why is he all chatty all of a sudden, I wondered?

Yvonne was cutting up her square of moussaka into itty-bitty squares. "Stella told me that she couldn't wait to go to Chile. She was very confident she'd get chosen."

"So Michael was true to form," I said.

"What a poseur!" Lorraine exclaimed.

"It's always been about him. Is he still on his safety campaign?" I asked.

"He never got the police crime tape he wanted draped across the copy room," Faye said. "Then he wanted to keep the door closed. He went on and on about how the copy machine was microwaving our minds. He's very much into radio waves burrowing into brains, you know."

"So that's w-what's wrong with us," said Dolores.

We fell silent as we finished eating our delicious gyros, souvlaki, moussaka, kota reganato, and salads. We sopped up all the juices with homemade pita bread. Hal and I walked up to the counter, ordered two Greek coffees and several slices of baklava to share with everyone.

The strong, sweet coffee set me off again. Everyone else looked ready for a nap.

"What did her son drop over her body?" I wondered.

"Godiva Pearls," Lorraine said. "I was standing behind him and saw the little can. He gave her a treat for the afterlife. Sweet dreams, mummy."

"Godiva Pearls? What are they?"

"Pearl sized chocolates,"

"That's creepy," Yvonne murmured.

"Would have been creepier having her c-cats stuffed and crammed by her side," Dolores said.

"All right. Enough. When did Stella cut her hair? Or did she? And the chocolate pearls are bizarre," Faye said.

Especially when they came from sonny boy, I thought to myself.

NINE

Everyone except Dolores gave me a hug when we left the restaurant. Why did I ever leave these dear people? I needed a life coach. They crossed Central on the way back to work, poor things. I walked up Central to cut across Johnson Field to my car. People were enjoying the large, green field where the football team and youth soccer camps practiced in the mornings. Dogs ran loose, jumped around their owners, chased balls and Frisbees, played with new furry friends, and did their business right under huge signs which read NO DOGS ALLOWED. I watched where I stepped as a few dogs ran up to me all slobbery but friendly. "Good doggie," I said to each one as I walked on. I was ready for my book and a nap.

I saw the open scissors sign for Steven's Family Hair Care on the corner of Central and Girard. I decided to take a detour to talk to Steven about Stella. I opened the door to his salon. At first glance Steven's salon resembled a waiting room at a hospital emergency room: A child asleep at his mother's breast, a bearded, shabby old man dozing while sitting up, two lovers embraced with heads on each other's shoulders, and a woman in a business suit working her smart phone. Steven was cutting a man's hair.

Well, he didn't waste any time! There was my inspector talking animatedly to Steven. Steven was laughing away cutting James's beautiful auburn hair. How special! When he cuts my hair Steven mumbles, stops to stare out the window, stops to take long phone calls, and one time stopped to flip through a magazine! They are certainly hitting it off! They did make a handsome couple. I'll have none of that, I decided, as I walked up to them.

"And then they asked me to model their line of clothes in New York for the American Independent Designer Showcase," Steven was saying.

"And did you?"

"I did, but it was punk street wear. I had to put magnetic piercings in my nose, ears, and lips."

"I can only imagine how you looked. How did you feel?"

"Like a wild and crazy guy."

"Ha. Did you have an adventure?"

Their conversation stopped when they saw me. The energy between them dropped.

"Caro," Steven said quietly after a pause. "Do you have an appointment?"

"Did you or didn't you cut Stella's hair," I blurted out.

"Who's Stella?" Steven asked.

I pointed rudely to James. "Hasn't James, Albuquerque Police Department's INSPECTOR James Hutchinson, asked you about her yet?"

"Are you really an Inspector? Cool!"

"So good to see you again, Mrs. Steele."

"I'm sure," I said. I pulled Stella's funeral service program with her pudgy face on the front out of my purse. "Her!" I put the program right up to Steven's face. He slowly walked over to the front desk. He slowly opened a drawer. He put on a pair of glasses. He slowly walked back. Steven drove me crazy. Why didn't he wear glasses when he cut hair?

"Oh her. Yes."

"When?" My voice had raised several octaves. I woke some clients up.

"What's the problem? Calm down," Steven said in a low voice. "She said that she wanted a cut and that you recommended me. Thanks."

"You're welcome. Did she say why she wanted all her hair off?"

"I appreciate you helping me with my job, Mrs. Steele," James said.

"Oh!" I exclaimed at James. I looked at Steven. "I don't understand! She always insulted me when I got one of your haircuts. She didn't like short hair. She said I looked like a man!"

There was a beat before both of them burst into laughter. Steven pulled several sheets of Kleenex from a box on a shelf. He gave some to James. They wiped their eyes. My face got beet red.

"What's so damn funny?"

"Oh Caro, you are so entertaining. Why would you ever take that comment seriously?" Steven drawled.

"Mrs. Steele, may I add, that you could never look like a man," James said.

"My feelings were hurt!"

"Of course they were," James said and nodded his head.

"Look, Stella said that she wanted a new look," Steven cut in. "She wanted to surprise someone. Also she said she was hot."

"Hot? Hot? Who's hot? The person she was going to meet, or she felt hot?"

Steven sighed, "She just said she was hot."

I took a deep breath. "How was her mood?"

"She was bossy but rather charming."

"Hmmm. OK. Sorry to interrupt. Thank you ever so."

"No problem, Caro." Steven started running his fingers through James' hair. I salivated.

"Thank you, Mrs. Steele," James said sincerely, I thought.

As I walked out I heard them start a conversation comparing the benefits of fish versus flax seed oil. They should have been talking about me.

TEN

I could not concentrate on *The Love Crescent* even though Jessie was devouring every inch of Pilar's body in a meadow of wild flowers at the foot of the Rockies. (Oh why doesn't he leave her alone, I grumped.) He cooked for her afterwards. (Oh give me a break, Tina, I silently pleaded with the author.) Jessie jumped up after their simultaneous (what else?) explosive orgasms, sprinted to a nearby stream, caught a trout with his bare hands, foraged for wild asparagus and mushrooms, and sautéed everything up in a pan of bear grease over a fire. With the ready supply of flour and sugar he always kept in his saddlebag, he whipped up a tart with blackberries he had picked before breakfast. Meanwhile Pilar cooled her *como se llama* in a bubbling brook. Enough. I sat down at my computer.

I Googled the Alma Radio Telescope in Chile. A BBC site reported that this was one of the grand astronomical projects of the 21st Century. It will enable astronomers to see events in the very early cosmos that are beyond the detection of current technologies. Key early targets will be the "birthing clouds" of new stars, and the discs of dusty debris that emerge around these newborns to produce planets. The world's astronomers have scrambled to be part of the early science observations. Almost 1,000 proposals have been submitted—far more than can be accommodated in the initial nine months of viewing time.

Hmmm, I thought. Would Hank Burns murder Stella over a proposal to study in Chile? More has to be at stake, surely. He would never bring her candy! Or perfume! Oh who knows what he would do. I remembered his dream was to build Very Large Arrays on the dark side of the moon. These could pick up wavelengths from outer space that were not distorted by water vapor in the earth's atmosphere. The Alma site claims to take our understanding of the universe to a new level. What was Stella researching? Stars, of course, but something else. Had to be. I searched for more BBC postings on Astronomy and found one where molecular oxygen, the one we breathe, was found in the dust of baby stars in the constellation Orion. There has never been this form of oxygen detected in space before. Was Stella part of this research team? And what did this have to do with murder?

I was getting an astronomical headache. Douglas was drumming in his room. Every cymbal crash shot pain through the fillings in my teeth. I was still stuffed from lunch but had to think about dinner. Wishing my husband would bring home the bacon and fry it up in a pan, among other things, I stared in my cupboards. I'll make tuna touchdown. I can hear my sons groaning now. It's amazing what I remember from seventh grade home economics class: one can of tuna, one can of cream of mushroom soup, splash of milk, chopped onion, grated cheese, crushed potato chips, and macaroni. I will not add a can of peas. I'll toss a salad later. Dinner was made. Where was Max? Little darling. I heard Douglas talking on the phone

in the garage. My house was quiet. Where was my husband?
I did not care as I sunk into his Finnish chair thinking of my
inspector. I wondered if anyone was fixing him dinner tonight.
What did he like to eat?

The phone was ringing. I opened my eyes. Max, Douglas and
John were standing in front of me.

"How was your day, Mom?" Max asked.

"What's for dinner, Mom?" Douglas asked.

"Funeral wear you out?" John asked.

"Ha ha! Jocularity!" I said as I reached for the phone.

It was Faye asking if I could come in to help organize new
reading material in the Physics and Astronomy library. "We
haven't been able to replace you because of the hiring freeze.
We need your help." How could I refuse?

ELEVEN

The dog sneezed. What was this aroma? Delightful! She un-curled from the pillow. She leaned over to rest her snout on the hand covering a book. She started to lick the fingers in a loving dog kind of way. Well, what a surprise, she thought. A loud snort followed by soft puffs of air coming between lips caught her attention. There was more surprise on the face! What a treat. Her tail thumped as she licked around the lips gently. All clean. The now wide-wake hound jumped off the bed. She rose up on her hind legs to follow the intoxicating scent on the end table. There was a pan with one spaghetti noodle hanging over the side. Forget that. Her nose sniffed a fork, a wine glass, and a bottle. Boring. A gold box sat on the edge. Very excited, she hit the box with her nose, and pounced on it as it hit the ground.   Carefully, using only her front teeth, she daintily lifted one morsel after another out of their individual pockets. Oh the joy of it all!   She frantically pawed the box and found a second layer of heaven. Delicious! Chew, chew! All gone. Too bad. She could have eaten these all night. She felt alive! But tired. She could not quite jump back up on the bed. The floor will have to do. She missed the cotton duvet with the peacock design and down alternative pillow but sank immediately into darkness.

TWELVE

Oh the bliss of parking at Physics and Astronomy on the University of New Mexico campus. Right near the building! Faye said she would have a visitor's pass for me until I could apply for the official one. I walked in the door at 8:30. So quiet. I looked through the main office partition glass. No Faye. Usually she was here at the crack of dawn. Yvonne sat pertly at the front spraying Lysol on her desk surfaces. The work-study sat at the center table looking into a compact mirror applying mascara. Maybe Hal had the parking pass. No Hal. I had to find Dolores. I walked through the office to the back door of the hallway where Dolores worked. Her door was cracked. I knocked.

"Y-yeah?" came a grumpy voice. I walked in.

"Hi Dolores," I said.

"So you came back? Glutton for p-punishment?" She bent her head over a sheet of paper and worked furiously on it with a stubby pencil. Her nails were bitten down to the quick. She wore the same animal print shirt, gray polyester pants, worn brown leather belt, and powder blue SAS shoes with the stiches unraveling around the toe. Why doesn't she buy new clothes? Dolores had degrees in accounting and astrophysics and should know better!

"Aren't we all?" I sighed and plopped down in a chair.

"Harrumph," she said and continued scribbling away.

I looked around her office. On the wall were two huge posters of blueprints for the Starship Enterprise. One was in English. The other one was in Klingon. A stack of crossword puzzle magazines was in her bookshelf along with accounting textbooks, astronomy textbooks, and the (BIG) Red Book of University of New Mexico Rules and Regulations. A McDonald's Senior Coke cup was on her desk next to an Egg McMuffin wrapper. There was a framed picture of Dolores's mother staring unsmiling at the camera. No make-up. Severe bun. I picked up the photograph.

"How's your mother doing, Dolores?"

"Not well." She put down her pencil. "I-It's very hard for me to know what to do with her. I can't do anything right. She is h-hateful."

"I'm so sorry. Alzheimer's changes people."

"Oh s-she's always been hateful. B-but it's gotten worse. I'm worn out."

"Have you thought about putting her in a home?"

"Do you know how much those places cost?" Dolores exclaimed. "I can't afford it! I do what I have to do!"

"At the expense of your own health?" I looked at her pale, pinched face.

"You do what you have to do," she repeated, emphasizing each word.

"Dolores! There must be places that are affordable. That take Medicaid! Call social services. They may help you--"

"Did you come in here to talk about my mother?"

"Well, no. I need a parking pass. What's wrong with you?"

"Everyone wants money, money, money! That's what's wrong with me!"

I followed her down the hall into the main office. She pulled a huge ring of keys out of her pocket and unlocked a drawer in Faye's desk. She handed me a large yellow cardboard rectangle with PandA VISITOR stamped on it.

"Thanks, Dolores," I said to her back as she walked back down the hall.

"She always ignores me!" Yvonne simpered. "She has a bad attitude!"

"Dolores has a lot on her mind. Where's Faye?"

"She called in to say she'd be late."

"Oh."

I went out to my car and stuck the pass on my dashboard. I was already tired. Why was I doing this, I wondered. I was going backwards when the universe moves forward. I was making a huge mistake! Maybe. But I did feel good getting ready to go somewhere this morning. I was getting frowsy and bored. I felt elated putting on eyeliner and wearing pants with a zipper.

As I reentered the building I saw Cecilia DeBlasi curled up on a sofa reading a book. She was in overalls, plaid flannel shirt, Doc Martens, and the usual bandana covered her lovely hair. She didn't look up. I went back in the office.

"Well, I'm here to organize the reading room," I told Yvonne.

"OK." She retrieved the ring of keys. I followed her down the hall.

"Where's Hal?" I asked.

"His bike had a flat," she said.

She opened the door to the library.

"Have fun," she smirked.

Musty, stale, dusty odors hit me. Study tables were stacked with journals, magazines, reprints, "to-go" coffee cups, soda cans, empty water bottles, loose staples, loose sheets of paper, books, and candy wrappers. So much for the No Food and

Drink Allowed sign on the door! Books were jammed into metal shelves all askew, some stuffed sideways with cracked spines.

"What a dump!" I exclaimed aloud borrowing shamelessly from *Who's Afraid of Virginia Woolf.* Unfortunately, there was no one around to admire my delivery. I must attend to these poor books first. I hated to see a mistreated book! I needed a dust cloth. I needed garbage bags. Hell, I needed Mini Maids! Swirls of sunbeams flew around the room reflected through dirty windows. I smelled a whiff of BO. I had to open these windows. I suddenly got the same anxiety attack I had in antique stores. I felt smothered by things old and used. This made me feel old and used. I hated that feeling. I shot out the door.

I ran outside the building through the double doors. I breathed in air filled with second hand smoke. A few morally bereft addicts were smoking by the corner of the building. They were laughing and having a great old time. I would have joined them, but I never lit up before noon. Instead I looked up at the clouds. "Get over yourself," I said and went back in.

I stood in the foyer looking at Cecilia. Her nose was in a book. She needed company, I rationalized, as I plopped down next to her.

"How are you, Cecilia?" I asked in a calm, solicitous tone.

She tilted her head to look at me. Her fair skin was scrubbed clean. A sprinkle of freckles covered her nose. Her blood shot, puffy hazel eyes stared unblinkingly into my puffy heavily made-up hazel eyes. Was she still crying over Stella?

"Why do you ask?" she murmured.

I had to think. "I was quite moved by your, shall I say, eulogy at Stella's service."

"Oh that."

"Well, yes, oh that, indeed! I didn't think you thought that highly of her."

"Yea." Cecilia started to flip through her novel. I was not to be put off. I tried flattery.

"And you looked positively stunning."

"Yeah?"

"Why did you defend her so passionately? Two years ago you told me that she did not pass you on your thesis. You were so upset."

"Stella gave me another chance. I'm not going to medical school now. I am applying to the University of Hawaii for a PhD in Astronomy. I want to continue Stella's work."

"How noble of you."

"Are you being sarcastic?"

"No! I truly admire anyone who studies astronomy. I wish I had the higher math skills to pursue the mysteries of the universe. I'm so proud of you." God, listen to me, what a patronizing twit.

"Stella believed in me. She was very hard on me and other grad students, but that's because people had been hard on her all of her life! She pushed us. That's the real world, she would say! Did you know that?"

"I knew about her family challenges," I said.

"I know you hated her."

"Did she tell you that?"

"You broke her heart--like everyone else in this department!"

"She became very toxic to me and all the staff."

"She had to fight. All her life she had to fight."

"I am honestly sorry that she was murdered. I would not wish that fate on anyone."

"Yea? Sure."

I stared at Cecilia as she bent her head over her book. Hmmm. *Game of Thrones.* What a slog. I tried some new patter.

"You really looked beautiful at the funeral. Very dramatic."

"Oh...that...."

"Oh...very rockin' that!" Me trying to be cool.

Cecilia smiled.

"I just came from an audition for *Cabaret* at Albuquerque Little Theatre."

"So you act, sing, dance AND study cosmic gas?"

"I try. My sister is an actress. She said I should have more art in my life."

"Wise sister. Have you heard anything?"

"No. Not yet. I don't expect to."

"Never say never! At least you were out there." Me the cheerleader.

"I'd rather be studying space: The final frontier."

"But it's good to get out of one's head and..." I started to babble.

Hal sprinted into the building. Cecilia jumped up. She ran to him and grabbed his arm. Hal looked down on her and whispered in her ear. He must have fixed his flat.

THIRTEEN

Faye still had not come in. I needed to know what she wanted me to do first in that Reading Room. I also wanted to know what was going on with good old Hal. I felt overwhelmed even though it was only 10:00. Seemed like I'd been here all day. I walked down the hall to the water fountain. Some professors shuffled by me looking at their shoes. A few hugged me and said kind words. It was nice to be appreciated.

I got the chills as I passed Stella's office. I remembered it being like a spider's web: dark, ghostly light coming from her computer screen, the sound of a humidifier humming, clammy air reeking of Knowing perfume, the red velvet chair in the corner, and ornately framed rather morose pussycat photos on the wall. Glow in the dark stars were stuck on the ceiling. Hershey candy wrappers and coke cans spilled over the trash-can. She played sound tracks from science fiction movies like *2001: A Space Odyssey* and *Star Wars*. Costumes swung eerily from a rolling metal clothes hanger. Masks and wigs were on a shelf. Her class would hoot and holler when she'd make an entrance as Princess Leia, Lieutenant Deanna Troi, Mr. Spock, or a Borg. She strutted around as Han Solo with a graduate student dressed like Chewbacca when I took that one class. Even though these were dated characters, the students raved. What a card.

I was happy to see Griselda coming down the hall behind her push broom.

"Chica!" She called out.

I ran to her for a hug. She felt my forehead. "What's wrong with you? Back in this place? Even I won't go in the Reading Room!"

"Everything's wrong with me," I sighed.

"You think too much, Chica!"

I started to cry. I felt like a baby. Griselda handed me a snowy white handkerchief.

"Be happy! Life is too short!"

I was about to reply when I saw Inspector Hutchinson coming towards us.

"Hello, Griselda…Mrs. Steele. What a pleasant surprise. Will you please let me in to Stella's office, Griselda?"

"Of course, Mister Inspector! And how are you today?" She dug a giant ring of keys out of her pocket.

"Just fine, thank you. And you?"

"Ha! The same! Fine and dandy! Sweet as sugar candy! I made that recipe you gave me for *ajiaco*. Delicious!"

"Glad you liked it. One of my favorites!" He turned to me. "Are you all right?"

I was stuck for an answer. "Yes. Oh yes." I finally said twisting the handkerchief.

Griselda unlocked Stella's door.

"Can I please go into her office, too, Inspector?" I asked.

"Why?"

Before I could answer Griselda linked her arm through mine. "We have something to do first, don't we?"

"What?" I exclaimed. Griselda grabbed her broom and pushed me like a hockey puck down to the bathroom. James watched us go.

"What are you doing, Griselda? I need to investigate!"

"Not until you clean up your face!"

I looked in the mirror. Black streaks ran down my cheeks. Gross.

Griselda reached in her fanny pack and handed me a small jar of Pond's Cold Cream. She ripped off some toilet paper for me. I wiped off the smudges.

"There! No more tears on your pretty face. The *bruja* is dead. Go have some fun!"

She swept me out of the bathroom singing *Besame Mucho*.

"You are very bad!" I said. "But I'll wash your hankie."

Griselda leaned back her head and laughed. She snatched the hankie out of my hand and twirled it over her head.

FOURTEEN

I couldn't wait to be in Stella's office with my Inspector. I had to find out if there were any developments on the case. Yea, right, I told myself. I saw Faye coming down the hall. Oh no. She stopped at Stella's door and knocked. James came out.

"So Griselda let you in? Sorry I wasn't here. Yvonne had run an errand. Lorraine was at Purchasing. Hal had a flat. Thank goodness the work-study answered the phones. This is a weird morning."

"Everything worked out," he said. "Something happen to your eyes?"

"Juniper allergy," Faye said abruptly. She turned to me. It looked like she had been crying for days. I could barely see her irises. And she was not wearing a barrette! "And how are you doing?"

"Well, I went in the Reading Room. It's worse than I thought. I'll need cleaning supplies and fresh air. At least I want the door opened."

"I don't know what we can do about fresh air. I'll talk to the physical plant people about the windows in there. Maybe an air conditioning duct is clogged. I'll take care of it. Just do what you can a few hours a day. I appreciate it. Thank you."

"You're welcome."

James excused himself and went back in Stella's office. I walked with Faye back to the Reading Room. It wasn't the direction I desired. Where was my backbone?

FIFTEEN

I abruptly turned away from Faye back to Stella's office. Her blackout curtains still covered the windows. I saw James in the middle of the room. He was staring at the ceiling. Something came over me. I was not myself. I closed the door. He looked at me. I pointed up. I turned off the lights.

We looked up as the stars and planets gradually turned blue-green. They covered us in that dismal office with a magical glow.

"Keep looking up," I said.

"Always," he replied.

The door opened. Faye turned on the lights. The Inspector and I turned away from each other. I had to say something reasonable. I saw all the shelves were bare.

"Where are her books?" I asked.

"In the Reading Room," Faye said.

"The family donated them to the university," James said.

"So kind, I'm sure. Which pile are they?" I asked. "There are so many in there."

"Does it matter?" Faye asked.

"I'm only interested, that's all." I was surprised at her snippy question. "Any novels?"

"Yes. *A Good Man is Hard to Find, Great Expectations*, and *The Story of O*," James said.

"Now that's an eclectic library! Are those in the Reading Room?" I laughed.

Silence.

Faye said, "I took the novels. Lorraine took the cats. Let's go, Caro, so Inspector Hutchinson can inspect."

I took one last look at my Inspector and followed Faye down the hall.

I kind of skipped behind Faye through a cloud of Youth Dew perfume. My nose started to dry out. Her tiny feet in beaded flats kept a rapid pace.

"So what's going on with Hal and Cecilia?" I said to her back.

She stopped suddenly and faced me. "What do you mean?"

"Well!" I got animated. "He walked in the door late this morning. I was talking to her. She jumped up and ran to him. He put his arm around her, and they walked down the hall."

"Oh she is so needy! I'm getting real tired of her. Hal is such a pushover. He's helping her transfer to the University of Hawaii. Lots of paperwork: Getting an assistantship lined up, Google mapping the area, housing...you name it. I don't know how she ties her own shoes. And she's getting a PhD! Academics! Universities are full of people who can't function in the real world. They are truly ivory towers!"

"It's nice to feel needed."

"I need him to put his butt in a chair and do his work, but who cares what I want."

"I do," I answered. "I'm here."

"Yes you are. Thank you." She put her arm around my waist. I felt warm, fuzzy, and tense all at the same time.

We reached the Reading Room. Faye unlocked the door but stood in front of it.

"Will you go to a canine CPR class with me this Wednesday night?"

"Say what?"

"A CPR class for dogs. You have a dog, don't you?"

"Well, yes...."

"Every responsible pet owner should know what to do if their dog stops breathing. It only makes sense. One never knows."

"I've never heard of this before."

"It's new."

My ears started ringing at this strange invitation. My mind was whirling. I knew Faye was crazy about her dog. He was like her child. Should I go? It's not like my career depended on it. What career? But her bloodshot blue eyes and unbound, wild curls made Faye look so desperate. What am I doing at night anyway? *The New York Times Crossword*, writing in my fear journal, hydrotherapy...

"I'll go."

"Good! I'll meet you at Good Samaritan Veterinary Clinic, on the corner of Wyoming and Menaul, at 7 PM on Wednesday." She walked away.

"Curiouser and curiouser," I murmured as I entered the Reading Room.

SIXTEEN

I wanted to find Stella's books. There were so many piles of books on tables and on the floor. I walked carefully around the stacks. I saw some texts covered in brown paper. Years ago students could get sheets of these book covers free at the bookstore. Then one had to measure, cut, fold (following very unhelpful red dotted lines with tiny written directions written along the sides) it over the book. My books always looked like I squashed a grocery bag around them and scotched taped it up. I didn't know Stella was old enough to use these book covers. Now nobody covers their $300 books. I picked one up, opened the first page and saw her name written in girlish curly, rounded cursive.

I heard a thump and a muffled "shit". I froze. Silence.

"Who's there?" I asked. I looked toward the tall shelves toward the back of the room. Oh just go over there, I thought. It can't be a mouse. First I propped open the door with a chair in case I started to scream. Faye can save me. When I turned around there was Hank Burns. He had dust in his shiny black hair and on his clothes.

"Dr. Burns…"

"Hello. How are you?" he said heartily full of bonhomie. I immediately felt suspicious.

"I'm fine, thank you. And how are you?"

"Fine, thank you."

Silence. He looked out the windows.

"So you are staying a while in Albuquerque?"

"Yes, doing a little research."

"How do you like New Mexico State?"

"Fine, great place."

"How are Claire and the twins?

"Just fine, just fine."

Silence. He looked at his shoes.

"What are you doing in here?" I asked.

"What are YOU doing in here, more like it?" he said in his booming professorial voice looking right over my head.

"Faye hired me to organize this Reading Room."

"Well, you've got your work cut out for you! Ha!" He said without smiling.

"It is a mess. You have dust all over you. You must have really been digging around."

"I was looking for something." He picked up one of Stella's criminology books.

"Can I help?"

"No." He started to walk out the door with the book.

"Excuse me, Professor Burns! Please leave that book!"

"Why? Do you want it? Are you going to enroll in criminal studies? Didn't like teaching, huh?

Snide bastard. "I need to process them for a gift donation receipt," I lied.

"Fine! Just fine!" He dropped the book on the table. He shot out the door bumping into the chair.

What a jerk. I walked up and down the bookshelves near the far wall. A pile of journals was on the floor. He didn't even pick them up! Why was he in the journal section, I wondered? They were all outdated. I did not want to think about him anymore.

I sat down in front of Stella's books and stacked the few covered ones in front of me. I opened to the title page. This can't be hers. The title was *Criminality and Its Discontents*. Whoa. I looked at another covered book: *Let's Get Free: A Cultural Theory of Justice*. What was she doing with criminal justice texts? I grabbed another one, flipped over to the front page of *Raw Law: An Urban Guide to Criminal Justice* when the tattered paper cover tore off the back. I peeled the paper off the book. I was wading it up to throw in the overflowing trashcan when I felt something hard. Inside the crushed ball of paper was a plastic card. It was scotch taped on the inside. I pried the small square off. It had a magnetic strip. A key card. To a room? An assignation? A memento of a night of bliss? I did not want to go there, but I had a flash of Stella rolling around with someone on a bed in an historic hotel, pitcher of margaritas and bowl of strawberries on the bedside table, sheets sprinkled with nacho crumbs, red underwear flung across the room, a travel Aveda candle flickering, the thick smell of bergamot and sex, neon signs flashing through the curtains....

A faint knock on the door brought me back to reality. I opened the door to see a bulky young man standing there shifting his weight moving from foot to foot like a mini march. I recognized him from the funeral. Stella's son, Brian. He did not make eye contact but looked somewhere over my shoulder.

"Heard Stella's books were in here. I want to go through them."

"Please come in," I said as he lurched past. He sat down in a chair and started flipping through pages of the nearest books.

"My name is Caroline," I said walking over to shake his hand. "I used to work with your mother."

He shook my hand while looking at a book. Great social skills, I thought. "Yeah? You have my condolences."

His hand was clammy. I quickly ran my hand over my skirt and sat down next to him. "And you're Brian. I have heard so much about you."

"I bet." He started putting books in different piles.

"Your grandparents still in Albuquerque, too?"

"Yeah. Cleaning out Stella's apartment. Taking care of death paperwork. They're here now meeting with the chair. Told me to amuse myself. Went to her office. Some lady with a broom told me her books were here. Wanted to see what she read, that's all."

Silence. Brian moved books around the table. He sighed.

"It's hard to lose one's mother, I know."

He finally looked at me. "She was never a mother to me. She always did what she wanted to do. I was in her way. Stella gave me up."

"Did she have a choice? She was younger than you when you were born." Brian stared at the books. "I'm sorry she was murdered."

"Someone had to do it."

I decided to ignore that. I looked at his swollen face covered with acne. He was overweight wearing baggy jeans, a White Stripes tee shirt, and untied high top dirty white leather tennis shoes. His nails were long. Greasy dishwater blonde hair hung in strands down to his neck. He was a fashion don't. I felt some pity.

"So!" I said gaily. "You're interested in criminal justice?"

"Dunno. Still exploring."

"Do you go to school?"

"New Mexico State."

"Oh! My brother went there. Excellent school. Do you live in a dorm?"

"No. At home with the old folks. Stella did not want to pay extra for room and board."

"I had to live at home when I studied at UNM. It's not the same, is it?"

"Can say that again." Brian stopped fiddling with the books. He leaned back in his chair and gave me his full attention. He had beautiful blue eyes. Something.

"Maybe you can move into a dorm or apartment with any inheritance you may receive."

"Fat chance! When I called Stella last month to ask for some money for a trip to Mexico City with my Spanish class, she told me that she would not give me another dime! And not to make any big plans if anything happened to her. All her retirement and life insurance was pledged to The Astronomical Society of the Pacific!"

"Oh she was probably just lashing out. Having one of her tantrums. Making you feel bad!"

"She sounded pretty serious."

"She was a good actress, Brian. What have your grandparents discovered completing all the university paper work?"

"Dunno."

"Well, don't think about that now! Your fears are not reality!"

"Yet."

Brian reached in his pocket. He took out a pack of Juicy Fruit. "Gum?" he offered.

"Gee, thanks," I said. We chewed together silently for a while. "So you like The White Stripes?"

"Went to a concert. They're awesome."

"My middle son is a musician."

"I played the trumpet in high school," Brian said while he stuck his head in a book.

"Are you taking any music classes at State?

"Naw…not part of my life anymore."

"It's good to keep art in your life."

Brian grabbed another book, turned to a page, put his elbows on the table and started to read. His signal to end the conversation. His foot jiggled. He popped his gum. I counted to 20 and took a deep breath.

"Brian, I have to tell you that your mother's living sorrow was losing custody of you." He stopped popping. "Stella and I had our differences--" He snorted and turned a page. "--But she talked very lovingly about you. She missed being in your life. She--"

"Hey!" He slammed the book shut and stood up. "You want to know how many times I saw MY MOTHER growing up? Exactly FIVE times from the age of 7 to 12! Let's see... that's once a year, isn't it? And it was just a visit. She did not even spend the night. Stella always came with a box of Godiva chocolates. We'd sit on the couch and eat them together. My grandparents usually left the house. I remember stuffing my face with candy and looking at her. Inhaling her presence. She was a stranger! But I wanted more of her. But all I got was her chocolate."

I got up. "Did you ever think, now that you're older, that Stella did not feel welcome in her parents' home? There were family issues that haunted Stella and caused her deep despair. Her absence may not have been about you. Stella was a wounded woman."

"Are you defending her? That selfish bitch?"

"Yes, she was a bitch, Brian, but that behavior did not grow out of a vacuum. I am not diminishing your grandparents or their love and care of you, but I wish they could have loved and cared for their daughter, too."

Brian burst into tears. I put my arm around his flabby waist. "Sit down. I'll get us some coffee. And Kleenex."

I walked to the narrow coffee room down the hall. I filled up two paper cups with the sludge that came out of the huge metal ancient coffee maker. I grabbed some cream and sugar packets and napkins to wipe up tears.

"No food or drink in the Reading Room," Lorraine deadpanned as she walked in.

"So fire me." I started to walk out the door without a glance.

"Well, don't you look all cute? Wearing a skirt? Are those little apples and pineapples?" She fingered my skirt. "How happy! And new flats? With a tiny silver buckle that matches your Tiffany silver heart bracelet? Nail polish? Expecting the Inspector, are we?"

I turned around. "Lorraine, I went shopping for the first time in a year. But not for the Inspector."

"Uh huh."

"Not all of us can pull off wearing black and white everyday," I said.

She ignored my vicious smack down. She spoke through her curtain of fried blonde hair and clenched jaw. "Inspector Hutchinson is paying a lot of attention to you but not for the reason you think."

"What's that supposed to mean?"

"Just what I said. He's looking at you very closely. Watching for a slip up. He still has your incriminating notes about Stella. Not to mention what the office staff witnessed the last year you worked here. He has interviewed us again. Or didn't you know?"

"Excuse me, Lorraine. I have work to do." I left.

"Oh Caro! I've missed ya like crazy!" she called after me.

"Yeah…right," I muttered. I hated to admit that I DID want to look better. I never knew when my Inspector showed up. I was feeling a little wild. With no place to go.

So James was interviewing the office staff again. He hadn't called me in a second time. I'm an open book, that's why, I assured myself as I walked down the hall. I expressed myself well the first time.

I kicked the Reading Room door a few times. Brian opened the door. He was not crying any more. I spit my gum into the trashcan. We took a few sips of hot strong awful coffee. He added sugar and cream. He sighed.

"I thought at last I could be free of Stella! My life could be lived without her walking on this planet earth casting an evil shadow on my grandparents and me. All my life I heard all these stories: Stella did not want me, Stella slept around, Stella wanted only success and power, Stella sucked everyone dry to get to the top, Stella was an ungrateful, mean daughter, if only her brother had lived, my uncle would have raised me, my uncle would have been good to his parents, Stella won't give us any money for your clothes…" Brian started tearing up again. "I grew up hating her."

"Yeah…" I took his hand.

"Did she really talk about me?" he whispered.

"Oh yes…oh yes. She loved you. She loved her brother. But she did what she had to do. She was driven." Listen to me, I thought. But I did believe all I said. And he was just a boy. I thought of my own sons. Their lightness of being. Brian carried such heavy emotions. He needed tenderness and reassurance.

Brian stood up. "I feel so guilty."

"Don't feel guilty, Brian. We are judged by our actions not our feelings!"

"Really?" He walked to the door.

"No books?"

"I don't want anything of hers."

"Take her love of knowledge with you, Brian." He walked out.

I collapsed into a chair. What lives we lead. What burdens people carry. I needed a cigarette. I fumbled in my purse.

"Organizing, Mrs. Steele?"

I turned around and there was my Inspector. What was this? Grand Central Station? I put my purse down and put on a professional face. I gathered my wits.

"You startled me!"

"What was Stella's son doing in here?"

"Just looking at her criminology books. He was upset."

"About?"

"Having a mother like Stella. Last month she told him that he will never get any more money from her even if she dies. She disinherited him."

"Damaged mother."

"I told him that she was probably just being dramatic. Do you know about her retirement, will, or legal situation?"

He took out his notebook and scribbled something.

"Hmmm…will he be all right?" He asked ignoring my question.

"Nothing that a few decades of therapy won't cure. So why does astronomer Stella have all these criminal books in her collection?"

"She studied Criminal Law at New Mexico State."

"What?"

"A long time ago. She changed majors, of course."

"I know that!" Really! I triumphantly held out the card. "Look what I found taped inside of a book cover."

James examined the key card. He smiled.

"Very good, Mrs. Steele. Show me the book, please."

I handed him the book with one hand and the tattered cover with the other. I even ran over to get the strips of tape. I wanted to help. James sat down and lightly fingered through the book and the thin cover. He peeled the tape off my fingers, one by one. I liked that.

"I think you should check this out," I said.

"Oh I will. Thank you. You have been such a help." He walked over to the trashcan and threw the tape away.

"Do you think it's a hotel key card?"

"I don't know. A lot of buildings use cards instead of keys for access. Some elevators are activated by cards instead of punching buttons."

"Oh." I could imagine Stella skulking down a hallway better than cavorting in a hotel room.

"I'll have the magnetic strip scanned. The information will be on there."

James took out a plastic bag from his pocket and put the card in there. "Good work, Mrs. Steele." He smiled. I smiled back then got all business-like.

"I think you should know that Hank Burns was snooping around in here," I said.

"Oh? Snooping?"

"Yes…and he acted suspicious."

"How so?"

"He wouldn't look me in the eye."

"I will make note."

"And he tried to walk out with one of Stella's criminology books!"

"Really? Which one?"

"*Criminality and Its Discontents*."

"May I have it, please?"

"Oh please do." I proudly handed it to him. He tucked the book under his arm. "How did you stop the professor?

"I told a lie."

"Not you."

"I am an actress."

"I bet you're a good one, too."

"I think you're making fun of me, Inspector Hutchinson."

"No, I'm having fun with you."

"Ah. But murder is serious business."

"There is a time for everything under the sun."

Oh a Bible reader. I looked at my watch: 1:00. "I have to go." I really didn't have to, but I wanted to sound like I had to. I was imagining having fun in an elevator with him. I may say or do something I regret. Or not.

"Will you be here tomorrow?" he asked.

"Yes," I said as I walked out the door, hopefully moving as a woman going to tango class instead of someone who was going home to let her dog out, have a BLT, watch *General Hospital*, and drive to Foodtown #2 for a chicken. And hug my children.

SEVENTEEN

Once home I fried up some bacon. I layered my favorite sandwich on toasted Rustic Loaf bread. Heaven. My soap opera was almost over. I was in a *Love Crescent* kind of mood anyway. I picked up the heavy manuscript. Munching along I turned to where I had left off. Jesse and Pilar were on a train travelling to God knows where. Oh yes, tracking down the villain who killed Pilar's mother, father, sister, brother, ranch hand, dog, and cat. (Pilar had a flesh wound and played dead.) After so much loss, Pilar was surprisingly perky, I groused. (Note to tell the author.) So choo-chooing along the Plains, our hero and heroine flirted, compared stewed rabbit recipes, locked the door to their compartment and got down to business. Their gentle rocking was in time to the train's gentle rocking along the tracks. (Oh God. Does anyone have rhythm like that? Maybe the author does. I started to dislike my friend intensely.) Jesse started explore her garden of delight. His tongue licked and probed gently. Pilar made yelps of joy which happened to coincide with the train's whistle. (Oh God.) I read on.

Jesse's tongue lazily moved to her quivering thighs. While concentrating on the inner, softest area his tongue encountered a rough spot. He licked again. Nubby. He outlined the uncharacteristically harsh texture with his tongue again and again. Pilar grabbed his hair. The whistle went off. Pilar screamed. Lifting his head out of her verdant garden and holding her thighs up, Jesse took a good look at the anomaly. Pilar fell silent but gamely did not mind being held almost upside-down. She was a limber woman. Jesse saw a crescent! A scar in the perfect shape of a one-quarter moon! (At last I knew where the title came from! Thanks, Tina!) *He drew his finger gently around the shape. Pilar groaned. "My neck," she whimpered. He lowered her delicious, Rubenesque bottom back down on the seat.*

"What happened to you, my lovely?" Jesse asked. His deep, basso voice broke.

"I was a child. I fell on tongs used to stoke our fire. I was nude. It hurt."

Jesse gathered her in his arms. They both wept over the injustices in the world. The whistle blew.

All right. That's enough. I dropped the tome down on an end table with a thud and went into the kitchen. I wondered if the Inspector was a Master Gardener or not while I took the fucking chicken I'd bought on the way home out of the refrigerator. I rinsed it off, dried it, and sprinkled it inside and out with pepper, paprika, garlic, onion, and celery salt. I stuffed it in a paper grocery bag, rolled up the end, put it on a cookie sheet, and threw it in the oven with some potatoes. Bag chicken. Dinner. Done. Now I have time to think about other things. Like how do you give a dog mouth-to-mouth resuscitation, and why did Stella hide a key card? Why did Brian feel guilty? And why did Stella study criminal justice? She never mentioned that to me. I still did not know why she cut her hair.

EIGHTEEN

"Stop fingering the chicken!" My husband yelled as Max flipped the chicken over and pried the "oysters" off the backbone. Max popped the juicy round morsels into his mouth. He looked at his Father while he slowly licked his fingers.

John turned to me. "Just once I want to eat my favorite part of the chicken!"

Jesus Christ. "Oh honey, you know you love the drumsticks best," I purred as I hacked away viciously at the carcass.

"Mom! I've asked you and asked you not to put tomatoes in the salad! I hate tomato gunk on my lettuce!" Douglas complained as he took his knife and noisily scraped all the tomatoes to the far side of his plate. He took a bite of white meat. While he chewed he tapped a lively beat with his fork against a glass of milk.

Max hummed as he took huge bites out of a thigh.

"QUIET!" my husband shouted. Beggar Suki ran out of the kitchen.

"I have a question," I said.

"Shoot," Max said.

"I found a key card hidden inside a book cover of one of Stella's books---"

"Souvenir of a fuck fest," Max offered.

"Language!" my husband said giving Max a strong disapproving fatherly glare. Max was oblivious as he threw a clean thighbone on the chicken platter and picked a drumstick. "And that's mine!" Max dropped the chicken piece with great ceremony and tore off a wing.

John turned to me. "Are you still obsessing about Stella's murder? Trying to solve it? Or trying to clear yourself? You know you did it."

"I think you did it!"

"Ha Ha! Never having met the bitch, she pissed me off the way she treated you."

"Language," Max mumbled.

"What did the key card look like?" Douglas asked.

"It was white with a silver magnetic strip."

"La Posada," Max choked with his mouth full of buttered potato, red chili, cheese, and sour cream.

Douglas jumped up from the table and went out of the kitchen.

I turned to Max. "How do you know what a La Posada Hotel key card looks like?"

"The church youth group went there on a field trip."

"Oh yea? The Calkins never told me they were taking the Youth Group to La Posada."

"Oh yea! We went to look at all the Santos in their *hijos*."

"I bet you did."

"It was a very holy time. Then Jim and I explored the hotel. We saw guests use a white key card to enter their rooms."

"Where were Mr. and Mrs. Calkins all this time?"

"Drinking margaritas."

"Well that's Eatcrustandpralines for you," John smirked. "Methodist chaperones drink tap water."

"Did it look like this?" Douglas said as he walked back in the kitchen holding out a key card.

"Yes! Where did you get this?"

"La Posada."

"Told you," Max mumbled.

"Now what were YOU doing there, Douglas?"

"Mom! You knew I had a gig in the lobby bar with the Highland Jazz Band! They gave us a room to change in!"

"Why didn't you use the lobby bathroom?" I asked.

"We had to store our instruments," Douglas said.

"I bet you did," said Max.

John boomed, "Mystery solved. From the mouths of babes!"

"Some babes," I grumbled.

NINETEEN

I have got to stop imagining. I have got to stop reading. I have got to ground both my feet in reality. This is my life I concluded as I dumped chicken bones in the garbage can outside the garage. I looked up at the night sky. Another mystery. I saw two bright objects side by side. They did not twinkle, so they were planets. Which ones? I'll go to the Observatory tonight and find out! I never cared for reality that much anyway. I will follow wonder any day.

I loved the campus observatory. I had not been there since 1986 when Haley's Comet streaked by. I parked in the spacious lot. It was dark and quiet. People moved almost reverently from telescope to telescope set up outside the building by amateur astronomers. The volunteers answered questions in soft, whispered tones. So peaceful. Even young children quietly stood in line to wait their turns to look. The universe was spectacular. I had forgotten how awestruck I felt surrounded by a blanket of stars. What a show. A really big show. I walked into the courtyard. I saw Dr. Gregory, the faculty advisor on duty, playing with his smart phone. Three white domes stood next to the high adobe wall. These were new. Must have gotten some money. Two were about eight feet tall with combination locks on the doors in front. The other was about five feet tall and no door. (I felt like a ferret walking around these domes almost sniffing.) I asked a student standing next to the open door leading to the huge telescope what they were. "Domes," he replied. (Thank God he didn't add "ma'am").

"Of course they are," I answered in dulcet tones. "But what's inside?"

"Telescopes."

Duh. I was brain dead. "Thank you ever so." I walked over to the green door leading to the slide room on the south side of the building. It was locked. Usually it stayed opened in the past giving slide shows to the public. Probably it was closed for the murder investigation. Perhaps in my feebleness I had the wrong door. Sixth graders ate my brain! But I did not see another door. I had to ask more questions, but first I wanted to climb up the winding stairs and look through the big telescope.

People started to leave. I looked at my watch. It was 9:30. The Observatory used to close at 10:00. I had time. I entered the observation tabernacle. Soft blue lights lit the way to the staircase. No one was in front of me. I heard two students on the upper platform near the telescope laughing. They stopped when I appeared. I looked through the eyepiece and saw a hazy cloud-like design in the midst of an ocean of stars. "What am I looking at?" I asked.

"Tonight we focus on The Orion Nebula."

"It's beautiful...but I thought I could see the two planets in the sky."

"Oh, Jupiter and Venus," one guy shrugged like it was an everyday experience not worthy of a telescopic lens.

"Well, yes."

"You can see them with the naked eye or with binoculars. But you can't always see the Orion Nebula. It's clear tonight. Perfect conditions."

"It's beautiful," I sighed. I forgot about everything in my life. I felt calm and one with the universe. I was stardust. Thank you Cecilia DeBlasi, Joni Mitchell, and, I had to add, Stella.

I heard the assistants shuffling around getting ready to close up and tore myself away from the heavens.

"What does the south green door lead to?" I asked.

"Astronomy 240 lab and the computer lab," one answered.

"There are no other rooms in the Observatory?"

"No."

"No slide room?"

"We don't use slides anymore," another said patiently.

"Oh! I thought--"

"Excuse me." I turned around and faced an old man standing on the step right behind me. He had a short gray beard and wore a fisherman's cap. He looked like Earnest Hemingway. "Why did you ask about that green door?" I looked at this person. Did I know him? Who knows anymore?

"I am just curious," I replied.

"Why?"

"A murder happened in that room."

"How was the person killed?"

"Strangled."

"Who was it?"

"An astronomy professor."

He abruptly turned around and hopped spritely down the stairs. I carefully walked down backwards holding tightly on to the rails. Damn clogs. I picked up speed once I hit the floor and race walked out to the parking lot. I looked around. He was standing in the courtyard, so I had to double back.

He said abruptly, "I was here a week ago. I heard loud voices coming from behind the green door."

"Did you tell the police?"

"No."

"Didn't you read about the murder in the paper?"

"I don't get the paper or watch TV."

"Radio?"

"Nope."

"A Zen master," I whispered.

"What?"

"Never mind. What did you hear?"

Graduate students were locking up. "Who has keys to the Observatory?" I asked one of the young men.

"Gosh. A lot of people. Right off hand I'd say two graduate students share one, although we have three on duty now due to the murder, the chair, Elliott the building supervisor, and every astronomy professor. Could be more. The police have already asked this question. Are you police?"

"Yea!" the old man said.

"No, no! I am no one. I mean, I'm someone, but really no one of consequence."

"You look like someone to me," the man said. I blushed. Thank goodness it was dark.

"Thank you all. Great evening!" I said to the students.

They smiled politely and continued shutting down.

I turned back to the old man. "Now where were we? Oh yes, you heard noises behind the green door."

"Laughter. Sounded like a party going on in there."

"What time was this?"

"About 9:30…I come to the observatory late to avoid the family scene."

"Hmmm."

"I thought it was strange to hear laughter here."

"Astronomy is serious business, for sure."

"And then the green door swung open and someone marched out and slammed the door shut."

"Man or woman?"

"Too dark. Could have been either. When the door opened, I noticed the glow of candlelight."

"Thank you, Mister…?"

"Call me Terry. And you are?"

"Call me Caro."

We shook hands.

"The police will want to talk to you. Can I give them your contact information?"

"No phone."

"Of course."

"I'm at the Observatory every Friday night if anyone wants to talk to me."

"Do you have a work phone?"

"I'm a writer."

"Oh really! I want to write! What do you write?"

"Have to go now." He walked quickly down the hill.

I called after him: "What's your address? What's your last name?" My questions dissolved unanswered into space.

The inspector needed to hear about my recent discoveries: La Posada Historical Hotel key card and the party on the night of the murder. Maybe I'll see him Monday. I can only hope.

TWENTY

Saturday dawned. Another weekend. John was outside doing yard work. I'll hear the usual complaints from Douglas and Max about the power mower running under their windows at 8 AM. I inserted my industrial strength imploding foam earplugs, sat in bed drinking coffee, and refused to even look at *The Love Crescent* manuscript on the end table. I did not need distractions. I should drive downtown to La Posada and show the front desk a picture of Stella or perhaps send the front desk attendant on a bogus errand while I flip through the guest book like they do in the movies. (Do guests even sign in anymore?) Why would La Posada tell me anything? I was indeed no one. The inspector had to flash his badge. If I had his card, I could call him to proudly share all my recent discoveries! Note to get his card. And why didn't the graduate students on duty the night of the murder mention a festive gathering behind the green door? Did they know about it? Note to talk to John Brooks and Katie Chu at work. The students staffing the Observatory are very busy answering questions and adjusting telescopes. Maybe they were not aware of Stella's little soiree.

They probably learned to stay out of her hair. Hahaha. Wasn't much left to stay out of that night. I could not believe how lightly I took her death. I was afraid of what kind of person I was turning into lately.

I reached over and pulled my fear journal and gel pen out of the drawer in the table next to the bed. I started to write: "I am turning into a snide, irritable, sarcastic, hateful, lusting in my heart, vengeful woman. What has a lifetime weekly church attendance done for me? Nothing? Do I only go for the show? I do love ritual. I do love singing. But I don't believe everything! I just feel good. Why can't I be good? Oh I am good. Too good. Why do I write that? I'm good on the outside and bad on the inside? Is my life one big act? A lie? Oh get off my back, Drama Queen! (I write on) I should forgive Stella for all her hateful behavior. And forgive and forgive. All these hurt feelings only weaken me. Like I'm drinking poison! Let them go, for Christ's sake. But I have to own my own feelings! I can't ignore them! My therapists said! And I read a quote from a book-- (Not *The Love Crescent*) (And by the way, why did I hold it against the author that she must have a wild sex life?) (Yet another fear that I have become envious and jealous)--anyway, in another book for my reading group, one character says to his brother: "You should pay attention to the people who irritate you." OK. I will pay attention to Stella. Why did she irritate me? Deep down she was out in public promoting the department when I wanted to. I love radio! I want to be in radio! Made me mad. She was on stage successfully teaching hundreds of students. I had a hard time with a class of 30. She was passionate about her subject. What am I passionate about enough to study long, hard years for an advanced degree? OK. I was jealous of her. Of her teacher of the year awards. OK. The truth is out. I did enjoy talking to her when she first came. She paid attention to me. A mere office worker. She experienced loss. But she went on. I admired that. I've tried to do that! Do I resemble her? Am I like her? I bounce into rooms with frantic energy like she did. I twirl around. I twitch. I'm loud! I always have something to say! I give thoughtful presents. She just was sharing perfume with me, for God's sake. I'm a lookist! (But I'm not rude!) Stella thought she was being helpful commenting on my hair. I hated her hair but could not be honest! Honest Stella! Oh Stella! Poor Stella! She did not deserve to die. All the awards in the world and academic accomplishments did not bring her happiness. She only had her cats. No one can be happy and lash out the way she did. She was desperate. Why? She had a good job. But I grew up in a loving family. No one took my children away from me. We all have our stories. I promised to be more compassionate in the future and not gleefully--

Max stumbled into the bedroom. I closed my fear journal. He collapsed across the bed. "French toast," he groaned. The weed whacker blasted outside my window. Hint, hint. Time to get up.

TWENTY-ONE

After frying a pound of bacon and a dozen slices of French toast for breakfast, I made a grocery list. I was so tired of planning menus: chicken something, Italian something, beans and chili, tuna something, pig meat something, tacos, steak, soups…oh God. Pots of food. At least we ate together at a table no matter how crazy the conversations got. We try. Or we're very trying as the old joke goes.

My new routine was to buy all my fruits and vegetables at organic supermarkets. No Foodtown #2 produce for my family! Who knows where they get their stuff? So I pulled into Sprouts Market and marched in piously with my reusable, biodegradable mystery material grocery bags with big flowers on the front. One dares not go into healthy stores without these bags. The first time I shopped there, the cashier rang up a basket full of food. "Do you need a bag?" she asked. Well, let's see if I can stuff everything in my purse, I wanted to reply. But I meekly said "Please." She tilted her head to the side, gave me a pitying look, reached under the counter and yanked out a brown paper bag. Horrors.

I fought my way through crowds of pale, badly dressed, pushy shoppers and surly green grocers stacking freshly picked produce as fast as they could from big carts blocking every aisle. I was so relieved to walk out of there with my purchases. I opened the trunk and loaded in my full bags. One tipped over. A cantaloupe fell out and dropped on the pavement. It kept rolling along in the parking lot. I bent over chasing it like an idiot. A pair of hands scooped up the melon. I straightened up. "Oh thank you," I started to say.

"Hello, Mrs. Steele. What a pleasure." My Inspector held out the fruit. I just stood there seeing my gawking reflection in his shades.

"This is yours, isn't it?" he asked still holding the bruised melon toward me.

I took it from him and clutched it to my chest. I couldn't breathe.

"So, you're a Sprouts shopper, too," James said.

"I am."

"So am I."

"That's nice."

Silence.

"Well, good to see you. Hope you have a good weekend." He tipped his head as a farewell and started to walk into the market.

"Wait!" I shrieked. I think I got into my head voice.

James rushed back to me. "Is something wrong? What happened? Are you all right? Give me that." He pried the melon out of my iron grip and put his arm around my shoulders. Stooped, limping, healthy shoppers stared at us. "Let's sit down." He led me over to the tables set up on the sidewalk where dour people were eating kale and quinoa salads and drinking wheat grass juice. "Sit. I'll be right back." He walked over to my car, tossed the melon in the open trunk, and closed it. He went into the store and came out quickly with a bottle of water. "Drink." I did.

"I'm sorry to frighten you, Inspector, but I have so much to tell you!" I exclaimed.

"Doing my job for me again?" he asked with a smile. What beautiful teeth.

"I do what I can. Anyway, the key card is from La Posada Hotel."

"I know. I scanned it at the department."

"Well?"

"Well, what?"

"Did you go to La Posada? Who was there? When?"

"I cannot say."

I looked at my reflection in his shades. I wanted to fling the water bottle over my shoulder, kick the table out of my way, and jump in his lap.

"So what else?" James asked after a long pause.

"I went to the observatory last night and met the strangest person. He heard me ask about the green door to the slide room. He told me that he heard laughter in that room the night of the murder. Then he saw a man or woman storm out at about 9:30."

"What's his name?" James whipped out his notebook.

"Terry. He doesn't have a phone. He said you could talk to him next Friday at the Observatory around closing time at 10:00. He looks like Ernest Hemingway. Can't miss him. Did the graduate students John and Katie say anything about a party going on behind the green door?"

"The students on duty mentioned nothing about a party. I'll talk to them again. Good work, Mrs. Steele. How do you feel now?"

"Much better. I just got so spaced-out with the runaway cantaloupe and seeing you. My discoveries were so exciting."

"This was a very exciting meeting." He removed his sunglasses and looked at me. "I am grateful for all you have done. How can I thank you?"

I could think of several ways. Most of them involved a key card. Let my organics putrefy in the trunk. Take me. Somewhere.

"Please keep me informed, that's all," I said coolly. "I really care." I had my honest sincere look on.

"One more question, Mrs. Steele. About Faye…she started working at Physics and Astronomy three years ago?"

"Yes, she moved here from Las Cruces."

"Makes sense."

"Why?"

"Faye graduated with a Criminal Justice degree from New Mexico State in Las Cruces."

"What? No wonder she told me to lock my car when I went to 7-11."

"Sound advice."

"She had just gotten a divorce."

"From a Ronald Ford. I know. He is a sheriff in Las Cruces. Did you ever meet him?"

"I did. He came into the office to talk to Faye about something. I thought he was a nice-looking man. He was polite to everyone. He looked older than Faye but maybe he was prematurely gray."

"Hmmm. When was this?"

"About three years ago. Faye had just been hired."

James scribbled in his notebook. Flipped through some pages. "Stella Cummings started at the department about the same time, I see."

"Why yes."

James closed his notebook. He smiled. So did I.

"So you've run checks on everyone," I said.

"Of course."

"Did you find out how boring my life has been?"

"I discovered that you are a very curious person, Mrs. Steele."

"Can I have your card?"

TWENTY-TWO

I drove home in a daze. I put my groceries away. John was starting a new carving project in the garage. He had made saints and birdies in the past. Now he wanted to start working on a huge tree stump our neighbor donated after having one of his trees taken out. John said that he was going to create fantastical beasties crawling out of the wood. But now he was sitting on a stool bent over staring at the stump with one hand cupping his chin, the other hand holding a lit cigarette. He resembled The Thinker sculpture: Planning his attack. Art is a process. Douglas was at band practice for the fall high school jazz festival. Max was God knows where doing God knows what. I hoped Peter called this weekend. Ever since he went to the University of Texas in Austin he has become so quiet. I missed him. I missed not having anything to do. I missed being useful. I missed a lot. I took Suki for a walk. I day-dreamed, looked in windows, and imagined everyone was happier than I was. What was their secret? They probably didn't think so much.

What was I going to do about Stella? How could I help find her murderer? I walked several loops around Hidden Park. I loved this park that was located in the middle of a square block of houses. Stately trees, lush grass, and several benches are surrounded by the backyards of homes where owners were hanging out laundry, gardening, or just sitting on lawn furniture drinking a beverage. A little, peaceful slice of life going on. I saw a Tai Chi class held in the middle of the park. Such beautiful movements. I saw young couples on blankets talking head to head. Runners and walkers moved around the outer dirt path. Dogs chased Frisbees. A father kicked a soccer ball around with his young son. Groups of women chatted while their dogs romped together. Suki did not play well with others. She was suspicious, fearful, and neurotic. Where did she get that?

Looking at my tense dog with her tail between her legs and ears stretched back flat against her pointy head made me wonder why was the Inspector asking about Faye and her ex-husband? And who will profit by Stella's death?   Faye's office chi will flow again. Hank Burns will not have a constant rival for research grants at Alma Conservatory in Chile. Her estranged son will not have to battle his mother for every cent he spends. Yvonne won't have to take so many phone messages. Lorraine won't have to make all of Stella's appointments. Dolores and Hal won't have a screamer in their offices.

On the other hand, I mused as I left the park through an alley, the department will miss her popular, cast of thousands class numbers and energetic public relations. Suki's tail and ears shot up. We were walking home. Well, somebody's happy.

TWENTY-THREE

I had to get another book to read. I can only take so much of *The Love Crescent*. My friend was waiting for my thoughtful critique. I had a list. But I needed a literary break. I parked on the neighborhood street next to Ernie Pyle Library. Ernie Pyle was a WWII war correspondent. He willed his home to the city of Albuquerque. It was a peaceful place: A small, white-shingled exterior with green trim with green, fluttering awnings. I could live there. On the south side of the library a spacious grassy yard spilled out surrounded by a white picket fence with a charming gazebo in the center. My pre-school aged boys gathered there once a week for reading hour, puppet shows and magicians. I missed those times. I walked in, smiled at the friendly librarian, and went straight to the revolving trays of new books. Ah! There was a new No. 1 Ladies' Detective Agency book! I could curl up with that and not get hot and bothered. I checked out a Lee Child Reacher thriller for John. I wished he'd get his own library card.

I loved driving home with new books to read. The sky was getting dark, clouds were coming in, and the wind came up from Africa. (Thank you Joni Mitchell!) I looked forward to reading all afternoon on my sofa with my blanket, my pillow, my dog, a cup of pear infused white tea, and John in the garage. Life was good. I turned my VW Beetle onto Central Avenue on the way home. I felt the wind buffeting my car every which way. Strong. I stopped at the light at San Mateo. I felt sorry for all the people huddled at the bus stop holding on to their hats and shopping bags. Nothing like bus stop people. Like a sub culture. I saw a woman wearing a long gray poufy coat with a hood. Dolores? All of a sudden I saw her careening backwards and hitting a traffic light pole. I clicked on my turn signal and pulled into the gas station behind the bus stop. I got out of my car and rushed over to Dolores. Dust flew into my eyes and mouth. Albuquerque weather!

"Dolores! Are you all right?" I yelled as she struggled to stand up straight.

"I just blew into a p-pole! Of course I'm not all right!"

"Get in my car. I'll take you home."

"I need to go to Walmart."

"OK! I'll take you to Walmart! Get in the car!"

"W-where is it? I'm not a mind reader!"

"I know! You're an accountant! Take my arm!" I shouted over the traffic noise and roaring wind.

We fought our way back to my car. I noticed her sole was flapping loose on her right SAS shoe as we ran. I folded her into the passenger seat. I got behind the wheel and started the car.

"Wow! Horrible out there!" I looked at her white face. "How are you?"

"I'll b-be all right once I get to WalMart."

"Let's motor," I said.

I drove down San Mateo to the huge Walmart parking lot. I dodged maniac drivers and jaywalkers. I swerved around RVs parked there for some reason. Scenic view? Charming.

"I'll drop you off at the door and park," I said.

"You don't have to stay!"

"I'll take you home, Dolores," I insisted.

She got out of the car. "I'll be in McDonalds."

"Of course."

What was everybody doing here? So many cars! I finally found an empty space. I jumped out of the car only to dodge very large people trying to control full shopping carts wobbling in the wind. I walked in, was greeted by a cheerful octogenarian, and turned left into the Walmart McDonald's. Dolores was sitting at a table eating a single burger. I slid in across from her.

"You know, Dolores, McDonald's is not real food."

"I like it."

"I know you do. It's not good for you. My sister went through a phase where she ate a lot of Kiddy Meals to collect mini-Beanie Babies, and she got gallstones!"

Silence. Dolores munched. "Well, you smoke."

"Right." I rose to buy a Diet Coke.

I sat back down. "So! What else do you like to eat?"

"I forget to eat at home."

"Wish I could," I murmured. "What does your Mother eat?

"Meals on Wheels."

"Well, that's nice."

"I g-guess."

"I'm so sorry about your mom. I can't imagine how hard it is to see a parent fail. And you have all the responsibility. Does your brother ever come down from Denver?"

"I don't call him. He's busy."

"So are you, girl!"

"I am doing what I have to do."

"You keep saying that."

"And I mean what I say. L-let's get a cart."

I thought Dolores was acting a bit crazy. She yanked a cart out of a line with surprising strength. I had to skip to keep up with her march down the crowded aisles. She threw Depends Adult Diapers and Fresh Wipes into the basket. She picked up a six-pack of canned Similac baby formula "She loves this cold in a tall glass with a straw. I s-squeeze a little Hershey's chocolate sauce in there." Dolores got little containers of pre-made jello and pudding. We shot to the Pharmacy department where she picked up a large container of Eucerine cream. "She g-gets so dry."

"Dolores!" I stepped in front of the cart and stopped it. "I don't know how you do all this alone. You need help. It's nothing to be ashamed of to call social services." She glared at me. I went on: "You know what they call Alzheimer's, don't you? The caretaker's disease. You may die before she does! Some nursing homes take Medicaid. No expense to you."

"I've looked at those places!" Dolores yelled. "They are like snake pits! I can't p-put her there! I want her in a good place."

"They're all horrible, Dolores."

"No! They're not! Look, I know you mean well. I've got this under control. Believe me, Caro."

"Are you going to get your brother down here to help you?"

Dolores yanked the cart out of my grasp, wheeled it around, and banged into a Dr. Scholl's display. Shoe liners, toe protectors, and bunion pads flew off their hooks.

"Watch out, Dolores! Calm down!" She stopped, bent down, picked up the fallen items and started hurling them at the nearby shelf of vitamins that made the bottles crash to the floor. Her face was beet red.

I stomped up to her. "Stop it now!!" I yelled in her face. Her eyes did not focus. She froze like in a trance. An "associate" appeared and looked at the mess.

"I am so sorry," I said. "There was an accident. I'll pick these up."

"Nooo problemoooo," the old man sighed. "I'll get some help. And thank you for shopping at Walmart!"

What a robot, I thought. Then I looked at the other robot. Dolores was blinking.

I said calmly, "Do you have everything you need here, Dolores?"

She shook her head back and forth no.

"What else do you want?"

Dolores looked at me like she just noticed I was there. She started charging down the aisles again to the paperback book section. We sailed past a huge religious section to the mysteries. Dolores tossed a Sneaky Pie Brown book into the basket.

"I like Rita Mae Brown," I babbled behind her. For someone so skinny, pale, and subsisting on McDonalds, she had energy. And how. "I've read her earlier books." I went on loudly to her back. "She has such a sense of humor and a sense of--" Dolores wasn't listening. We careened into a check out line.

I drove up to the entrance, got out, opened my trunk, and Dolores put in her purchases.   I watched her carefully. She seemed her normal odd self. As we turned out of the parking lot, I asked, "When are you going to learn to drive?"

"I know how to drive. I just don't want to. Buses are fine."

"Oh! I didn't know. Inspector Hutchinson takes a bus," I started to get all-conversational like she was a girlfriend.

"Harrumph," she replied. Then she looked at me. "You s-sure know a lot about the Inspector. Up close and p-personal? Buttering him up?"

"What?"

"Distracting his suspicions about you with feminine w-wiles?"

"That's ridiculous, Dolores! He's a nice guy, and we've had some chats, that's all. Besides, I don't have feminine wiles! That's so 19th century. And I'm a mother and long married--"

"And a prime suspect."

"You believe that?"

"Stella's the reason you q-quit your job. Throwing you into a profession that made you m-miserable. You're the only one of the staff who e-ever confronted her. She was on your back constantly. I'd see your face get so r-red when she walked behind your desk. You hated her."

"All true, Dolores, but I could never kill anyone."

"Harrumph. T-the more you rejected Stella, the stronger she pushed you until…."

I had to change the subject. Talk about pushing a person! Dolores was a master. How dare she accuse me! Crazy nutbag! I took a deep Yoga breath. I was a reed.

"Dolores, you really need some new shoes. Those are not good for your feet! The soles are gaping and--"

"They're just fine. I am saving money right now." She crossed her arms, turned away from me, and looked out the window.

"That's never been my strong point," I laughed. All confidential.

Dolores whipped around to face me again. "Of course not! Y-you have a husband to support you! You have never had to worry about money in your l-life! I fall asleep worried about m-money! I w-wake up worried about money! In between, I dream about money!" She jerked back to look out the side window.

I wanted to scream to the back of her hideous Medusa gray head that I have had worries in my life that she has never had to face in her wildest dreams. I've raised children. I've lost loved ones. I'm married. But what was the point? One cannot change another person. I couldn't get inside her head. Thank God. I will be kind.

We pulled up in front of her house. The front yard was all dirt. Dead ivy vines scrawled up the front of the house. Dead shrubbery lined the sidewalk. Everything looked dead. I turned to Dolores.

"I'm sorry to be the Grand Inquisitor today. I know you have a lot on your mind. I have to say that I haven't seen you for two years, and I am worried about you."

Silence. Dolores now stared straight ahead. I braced myself for another outburst. Silence.

"Can I help bring in your bags?"

Dolores turned to me. "No."

"Well, let me unlock the trunk."

"Now that's a help!" She finally laughed.

I watched her walk up the driveway hunched over with her bags. I waited until she opened the door. She dropped one bag and waved good-bye to me before she picked it back up and stepped in.

I felt so thankful to be going back home to my colorful, semi-dysfunctional family. I wondered if I should mention to Faye that Dolores needed help? But Faye seemed to need help, too. Oh we all needed sleep therapy in Switzerland!

I ordered take-out burgers and fried wontons from Lucky Boy for dinner. The boys stuffed them down and ran out to do their thing. Douglas had a date. Max was hanging out with a neighbor friend doing God knows what. John and I watched some TV. He fell asleep in his chair. I should have suggested a game. We could have played Scrabble or strip Crazy Eights? Too late. I hauled *The Love Crescent* manuscript into bed with me after a long, hot bath. I couldn't help it. I entered Tina's creation thinking all the while of another. I read:

Jesse and Pilar hopped off the train in San Jose. They too lusty breaths of fresh air. Their cheeks were rosy, and their rapid trotting steps down Main Street reflected how they were buoyed with anticipation of finding the dastardly murderer of Pilar's beloved, late family. But first they had to find a room to bathe and change out of their traveling clothes that were covered with soot and various sticky substances. Jesse entered a saloon to inquire about an inn while Pilar waited demurely outside with their bags. Jesse also wanted to show the wanted poster to saloon patrons. When Jesse finally came out, he found Pilar surrounded by men. She was laughing merrily and twirling her finger around one lustrous black curl that had escaped from the thickly coiled bun at the base of her snow-white neck. "Excuse me," he bellowed as he wrapped his tanned, muscular arm around her tiny waist. "Oh hi!" Pilar gushed. "Such friendly people here!" The crowd of men parted as Jesse swept Pilar off the saloon porch and down the street to the Dew Drop Inn. He carried both bags in one strong arm.

"Do we have to walk so fast, my love?" Pilar gasped, her tiny feet barely touching the dusty road.

"We must bathe," Jesse said through gritted teeth.

The management lugged a huge metal tub upstairs to their room and started to heat water to fill it. As this took some time, Jesse told Pilar what he found out in the saloon while he undressed her slowly behind a folding curtain.

"A man with an eye-patch, scarred cheek, pronounced limp, and three fingers on his left hand was here yesterday. He was looking for the home of a Zane Parker. The bar gave him directions to Zane's homestead." Jesse buried his head in the lace petticoat he had slipped off Pilar.

"Do you think he's there now?" asked Pilar in a muffled voice since her face was covered in the dress Jesse was pulling over her head.

"We will have to wait and see," Jesse said as he started to untie the many corset ribbons.

"My hero," Pilar sighed as she sank into the tub. Jesse plopped in facing her. Bath water splashed over the tub in undulating waves.

"A man's gotta do what a man's gotta do," Jesse mumbled. He leaned over and bit her glistening calf---"

Enough! I turned out the light. Can't a girl even relax in her bath? I must be getting old. I heard the door front door open. I saw Max lurch by my cracked door to his room. He was safe.

At the communion rail on Sunday morning I prayed for guidance and peace that passes understanding. I gave thanks for all my blessings. I prayed for Stella's soul and for Dolores. Then I joined my fellow raucous choir members and sang my heart out.

TWENTY-FOUR

My husband was mooning around. His jaw was jacked. I could tell by his lips that were often pressed into a thin line. Lately he did not even fall asleep in his Finnish chair but stayed up all hours watching the SyFy channel and eating bite-sized KitKats. I knew he was hoping to see Gamera, the giant flying turtle. His favorite. I had to do something. Be a good wife, for once. John needed attention. I did not feel like doing anything physical or making him Indonesian chicken or ironing his shirts, so I asked him out for a date. Maybe I could enjoy myself, too. Where there's life, there's hope, I hoped. I suggested the Martini Grill. John arose from the soft, green leather, took off his yellow checked drawstring pants, Bat Boy tee shirt, and kicked off his Crocs. He put on black jeans, an olive green plaid shirt, and black leather Van's tennis shoes. I met him at the door in black skinny pants, a plunging red blouse that showed my meager cleavage because I put on an underwire bra, and La Duca black leather heels. I outlined my eyes in blue glitter. John said "wow" when he saw me. His lips resumed their soft, full shape. We cleaned up pretty well. I was going to be charming company.

"We're going out!" I bellowed to Douglas and Max. Douglas had music blaring behind his closed door. Max's room was quiet. I opened his door. No Max.

"Where is he?" I asked.

"Who knows," John said. "Let's not try to know. Let's go!"

Entering the Martini Grill was like walking into an opium den without the opium. It was deliciously dark, smoky, and dimly lit by red exotic seashell wall fixtures. The booths were red velvet. I always felt decadent there. The wait people were either beautiful, provocative-looking women with whiskey voices, or drop-dead handsome young men with whiskey voices. Breathing in all that second-hand smoke, I guess. An elaborate, mirrored marble bar stretched across one side of the room. A tattooed bar tender in a wife-beater black tee and spiked pink hair worked her smart phone.

We sat across from each other in a back booth. John reached over with his hands open. I took his hands. He squeezed ever so gently and did not let go. His warmth spread up my arms.

"I have been so upset..." he began.

"Oh honey! I've been in quite a space lately--" I interrupted.

"I want to talk about me! I have been so upset. Caro! What's happened to you? To us? Your wild antics are affecting our family. Affecting me! I look in your eyes, and you're somewhere else. Do you even like me anymore? Tell me what I can do to make you happy. Just--"

"I have not had any wild antics, John," I said and withdrew my hands. I lit a cigarette. "I'm going through a transitional time right now. I'm thinking, that's all. It's not you!" His face got that stony look. His lips thinned. He was so sensitive! I grabbed his hands again. I remembered how he took me out for gin and tonics every Friday night when I student taught and could not stop crying. I wore big shades. Then we'd go bowling. He made me laugh until I cried again but with the silliness of life. John used to fling the ball down the alley balancing on his right toes with his left leg straight out behind him. He looked like a deranged statue of the god Hermes. I must have pity on his state of mind.

"Let's talk about something else," I started all up beat. "Like…how's the bag pipe band going?"

"I don't want to talk about the pipe band, Caro."

"What can I get you?" Finally, a drink! I looked at the waitress. Sweet Cecilia! She was wearing her funeral attire minus the embroidered hankie.

"Cecilia! Hello! I didn't know you worked here! This is my husband, John," I babbled. John stared with open mouth.

"Just started. I need to save money for Hawaii," Cecilia said.

"Well! You look great! John, Cecilia is a graduate student at Physics and Astronomy and aspiring actress! She just got accepted to the PhD program at the University of Hawaii."

"Congratulations," John said and broke into a smile. Oh good, I thought. Fleshy distraction!

"I'll have a Grey Goose martini up with a twist," I said.

"Same for me," John choked staring at Cecilia's huge breasts.

"Anything from the kitchen?"

I ordered a chicken quesadilla and spinach salad for us to share. Cecilia scribbled down our orders and pranced away saying "nice to meet you" to John over her shoulder.

"Nice to meet you, too!" said John leaning out of the booth to watch her walk away. "Wow," John said for the second time tonight. "She studies physics and astronomy?"

"Astronomy. But she looks so different at school!" I started in with my gossipy voice that gets John's attention every time. He can be a bitch. "She wears huge overalls, baggy shirts, Red Wing boots, and an old blue calico bandanna over her head."

"Covers that beautiful hair and…body?"

"Yes! It's a puzzlement! I tell you!"

We got head to head while I whispered, "And she was very close to Stella. Then Stella screwed her over on her comps."

We broke apart when Cecilia brought our drinks. Oh sublime martinis! A thin layer of ice floated on the top.

"I didn't spill a drop," Cecilia said as she placed them in front of us.

"God bless you," said John.

They were filled to the brim so we leaned over to take our first sip. Heaven. I felt warm and cozy at last. My marriage needed booze and cigarettes. Sad thought, indeed. Maybe.

The Grill was filling up. A few men sat at the bar. I enjoyed watching the bartender work so smoothly and quickly. An art. Like a dance. John was asking me more questions about Stella and Cecilia when I noticed a shiny black head on top of a short rounded back sitting at the bar. I looked in the mirror to see his face. Hank Burns! Oh dear God.

"John! Hank Burns is sitting at the bar!"

John turned around. "Ha! Your favorite person! I thought he went down to State?"

"He did but came back for Stella's funeral. Oh damn! Don't look anymore!" John had been to several department parties with me in the past and had met the professors. Probably Hank could not recognize John after so many years. And he certainly would avoid me if he saw me tonight. I stopped worrying.

We finished our martini. Cecilia brought our food. We ordered another drink. Thank goodness we were seven blocks from our house. We could crawl home if need be.

We ate the delicious quesadillas: triangles of flour tortillas filled with melted cheese, chicken, and green chili. We dipped them in sour cream and salsa made with fresh tomatoes, onions, chilies, lime and cilantro. We chewed our spinach salad tossed with lemony vinaigrette, chopped hard-boiled eggs, feta cheese, red onions, and bacon bits. We guzzled our vodka. It was nice. Until John said:

"Oh let's invite the poor professor to join us."

"Please, don't! He's not poor!"

"Can't you let bygones be bygones? You hold grudges like a Macedonian! Here is now!" Damn vodka! Made John expansive. "Come on, Caro." I could not shut him up.

"This is our time, honey pot. Please." John was doing this to torture me. He had his ways. Pay back time.

"Dr. Burns!" John called out and waved.

Hank turned around. For a nanosecond he recognized me and squinted his eyes evilly then broke into a huge fake smile. He picked up his pink drink, jumped down off his stool and slithered his way towards us. John moved over to make room. Hank squeezed in.

"John, right?" Hank said shaking hands with the traitor.

"Frank, right?" John said.

I died. What an ass. Both of them.

"HA, HA, HA!!!" Hank boomed. "I guess you heard about the typo your little wifey made!"

"Oh did she feel horrible about that!" John shouted. "Didn't you, little wifey?" Then he winked at me!

"Yeah, I felt horrible, Butt," I winked back at him.

"HA, HA, HA! Aren't you two a fun couple!" Hank exclaimed.

"We're a million laughs," I said.

"So! What have you been up to, professor?" John asked all chummy. He was killing me, that one.

"Well, I am on my way to the *Alma* Observatory in Chile. Got a grant! It was tough, for sure. But I was determined!" Hank puffed up his scrawny chest so the blue letters ALMA OBSERVATORY smoothed out over the pocket of his golf shirt.

"Why go to Chile?" John asked. Oh here we go.

"Maybe you don't read the papers, husband dear, (John hit himself on the side of the head like a dork) but Alma Observatory is making a chemical map of the universe starting the whole new science of Astrochemistry! Its nine antennas search for the building blocks of life! Chemicals in space! It collects 800 gigabytes of new data each day!"

"No shit," John said reverently.

"Yes," Hank went on. "Nature is cleverer than we are, my friend. But we mere earthlings are trying to solve her mysteries. Are we alone on this Planet Earth? I think not."

"*Alma* means soul in Spanish," I said. "Alma Observatory is looking for the soul of the stars."

Hank wiped the smile off his face and looked at me. "Well, aren't you the one."

"I read," I said with my mouth full of spinach. "And Stella told me."

"Stella had delusions of grandeur." Hank said in a flat voice. "She was all over the place with her research. What did she know about anything except how to promote herself? Her scientific method was a patchwork of fact and fiction. She should have been a science fiction writer for all she contributed to academics. She would stop at nothing to get what she wanted---which was a position at Alma Observatory. This time she went too far. Stella was a poseur and a lightweight. She never had the discipline for real study or the patience for observation which is the foundation of astronomical---"

"You astronomers!" John broke in. "No guidelines! Always searching! The sky is no the limit for you! Now CPAs have rules and regulations."

"But no *alma*," I snarked.

"HA, HA, HA! You two!" Hank barked.

"Excuse me," Cecilia stood at our booth. "Anything else I can get for you? My shift is ending soon."

"We're ready for the bill." John said.

"I'll have a cosmo," Hank said. "Going to another funeral, Cecilia?"

She curled her lip and walked away.

I was not having fun.

"Gotta pee," John announced. Hank got up and let him out of the booth. Then he sat next to me. My skin crawled. Cockroaches.

"So you and Stella had a little discussion about Alma?" he said. The whites of his eyes were shot with red veins. Up close his black hair looked like it was coated with shoe polish. Sweat beads lined his widow's peak. His hands were small, plump, pale, and smooth like a young girl's except for the inky black curly hairs that sprouted out of his knuckles.

"Yeah. Two years ago." I scooted away from him to the wall.

"Yeah? And?"

"She was excited about it being built. She wanted to go there when it was finished."

"I bet she did. Fat chance. Stella did not have what it takes, Caro. I did."

"Obviously."

"Obviously, nothing! I worked hard. Nothing obvious about it," he gritted his teeth. "When I found out she was competing with me, ME, mind you, (Hank banged his fist on the table) I knew she would stop at nothing to win." He brushed a tortilla crumb off the front of my blouse. I blew smoke in his face. He coughed as he eased closer and put his arm around me. "But let's talk about you. How are you, little librarian? Trouble in paradise? Having couple time? What's with the outfit? Not your usual Gap gear. Hoping to light a fire? Your husband tries so hard."

I shrugged his arm off. "Just like you." I reached for my drink and knocked my water glass over on the professor. "You're drunk."

Hank jumped up to get a towel from the bartender. He sat back down next to me, gave me a wolfish grin, and dabbed water off his Alma Observatory golf shirt. I was never so glad to see John return to our booth. He gave me a look. I held his gaze. He understood my distress, thank goodness. A perk of the long married. Usually. Something.

"Time to go!" John continued standing. "Early day tomorrow."

Hank did not let me out.

Cecilia plopped a cosmo in front of Hank so strongly that the drink sloshed over the top of the glass. She handed John our tab. She waited while he fumbled for his credit card.

"Let me out!" I said.

Hank made a big production of wiping up Cosmo puddles with his towel. He finally got up, and I got out. "You're too sensitive," he hissed at me. He sat down. He stared straight ahead.

I stood there while John still couldn't find his card. I watched Cecilia brush her lustrous curls behind her ears. I still could not believe she hid her crowning glory under a faded bandanna. Silence. John was ratcheting, Hank was sipping and dripping, Cecilia looked at the ceiling.

I needed to fill an awkward moment. A nervous habit of mine.

"I love your hair, Cecilia! It's so healthy and shiny," I said.

"Oh thank you, Caro!" She perked up.

"Do you use any product?" I asked her.

"Yeah…semen," Hank smirked.

Cecilia took John's card and told him to meet her at the cash register. She turned away without a glance. John put his arm around my waist, and we silently walked away from Dr. Burns. John's hand felt so good. So clean.

"I am so sorry, Cecilia," I said while John signed the bill.

"Oh that jackass. He's a mosquito to me. I'm just sorry Stella had to deal with him. He made her life miserable."

Back home, a trifle buzzed, I clung to John.

"He is a nasty little man," John said. "Me and my big mouth asking him over. I was not thinking of your feelings."

"I haven't been thinking of yours, either," I cooed all the while thinking about the pleasure I will have telling my Inspector about Hank Burns.

"I love you," John whispered in my ear.

"Me, too," I said and blushed with shame.

Max stumbled out of his room. "Any leftovers?"

TWENTY-FIVE

What I do for Faye. Doggie CPR class. I don't know about her.
I pulled into the St. Francis veterinary clinic Wednesday night.
I buzzed the locked door. A tall woman with a kind face and
sensible shoes opened the door for me. She introduced herself
as Dr. O'Brien. We walked through the empty waiting room
decorated with animal posters and down a hall to the surgery.
Faye was there. She hugged me tight. I could hardly believe
her faded jeans, wrinkled red Lobo t-shirt, and scruffy tennis
shoes outfit. Her curls were pulled back in a frayed scrunchie.
I felt sorry for her. She looked so vulnerable. On the operating
table was a stiff terrier dog on its back, feet in the air. I thought
it was a real dead dog at first. I freaked. But recovered. The
doctor put on a lab coat.

"Let's get started. I guess you both are the only ones coming tonight," the vet said.

Faye and I stood at attention near the table.

"Seeing one's dog go into respiratory arrest is a scary thing.
Luckily studies have found that human cardiopulmonary resuscitation techniques often work on our precious canine com-

panions. We must do everything we can in the moments following an accident to save our loved one."

Faye and I bobbed our heads in agreement. Faye reached in her pocket for a Kleenex. She wiped a tear from her eye. I stared at her. What was going on? What's wrong with her?

"Now we begin," the doctor said. "Try to find a napkin, a clean rag, your shirt perhaps, or a tissue to place over the dog's nose and mouth." She draped a white square over the stiff's snout. "Hold the nose. Now blow into the nose like so." The doctor put her mouth over the covered nose and started to noisily breathe gusts of air into the cloth. "Do this five times in quick succession. Then palpitate the chest as so." She clasped one hand over the other and started to press on the dog's chest. The body bounced up and down with each push. The legs waved in the air every which way. I started to laugh. Both the doctor and Faye gave me a withering look. I bit the inside of my mouth until I tasted blood.

"Repeat this several times until the dog hopefully revives. Now you try." Dr. O'Brien draped a clean cloth over the nose.

Faye stepped forward. She did an excellent job. Then she patted the stuffed dog's head. A fresh cloth was applied. I thought I was going to start giggling. This was a Kafkaesque experience. I can and I will act my way through this, however. When I put my mouth over the nose, I gagged. Tears filled my eyes. I looked up for some guidance.

"Not so much nose! You don't have to put the whole thing in your mouth!" The vet tut-tutted.

I put my lips over the nose and started puffing. One. Two. Three. Four. Five.

"You must give more air! More effort, please!" I was failing.

I returned to the nose and huffed and puffed until I got dizzy. I looked into the dog's glassy brown eyes. Dear God I'm going to faint. But I stood up and administered the chest palpitations like a trooper. Live Spot Live! I repeated silently without going into hysterics.

"Now when your pet hopefully revives he or she will be weak and frightened. Retire to a quiet environment where there is no stimulation. Offer water but no food for twelve hours. If the dog goes into convulsions take her to an emergency veterinary clinic. If after repeated CPR procedures the pet does not respond, well, the pet is dead. But you will have done your best! Any questions?"

"What about possible brain damage?" I asked.

"Always a side-effect. You may have to live with a special needs dog."

"I already have one," I said.

Silence.

After thanking the doctor profusely Faye and I walked out to the parking lot. She lit a cigarette with shaking hands. I joined her. We both looked up to the night sky that was clear with a blanket of stars.

"Hope it's this clear this Friday for the Observatory crowd," I said after a long silence and watching Faye light another cigarette off her first one. She just looked at me. Unfortunately, I started to babble.

"The donations must have dropped since it has been closed for the murder investigation for two weeks." Faye stared at me. I was beginning to feel uncomfortable which only made me talk more. "There was a big crowd there last Friday when it re-opened. I was there." Faye lit another cigarette. She walked over to her car and leaned against it not breaking eye contact with me. The lights went out in the St. Francis Clinic. The parking lot was dark except for the glowing ember of Faye's third Marlboro Light. The red tip reflected eerily in her glasses below her huge baby blue eyes.

"I met the most unusual man there! He said that he heard laughter behind the green door the night of the murder. I called him a Zen Master because he has no car, no TV, no newspaper, no---"

"So you were asking questions about Stella's murder?" Faye asked as she ground her cigarette out under the heel of her shoe.

Like a puppy wagging its tail, I thought Faye was pleased with me, and went on with great animation.

"Well, no, but I was asking an attendant about the green door, what did the department use the room for now, etc., and this odd man came up to me and asked me why I was asking, and I told him about the murder, and he told me about the laughter and that he saw someone run out of the door and---"

"Who did he say ran out of the door?" Faye stood up straight.

"He didn't know if it was a man or woman. It was dark, you know. But I told Inspector Hutchinson about this, and James will try to meet him at the Observatory this Friday for questioning, because the Zen Master goes every Friday night late to escape the crowds, and I couldn't have James call him because he doesn't have a phone, and--"

"Thank you for coming with me tonight," Faye said abruptly. "I needed to know how to do this." She turned back to her car. I switched gears skillfully.

"Did you lose your dog?" I asked.

"It's horrible to watch a living thing die before your eyes," she whispered.

"I'm sure." I said. "I'm sorry. We have had our old dogs put to sleep. I can never watch. My husband holds them."

Faye walked up to me invading my personal space. I took a few steps back.

"You know I could never have children. I've thrown all my love onto the dogs in my life." Faye spoke through clenched teeth. "My husband could not accept the fact I could not bear him children."

"I'm so sorry," I said again.

"Some people take advantage of another's weakness. They find out and plot their own selfish agendas at the expense of decent people. I find that cruel and unusual."

"Awful," was all I could say.

"Did you know Stella was pregnant?"

"What?"

"Remember when she called Lorraine to her office a few days before she died? Lorraine found her standing in a pool of blood. She was having a miscarriage."

"But she was old! I mean, how do you know?"

"My neighbor works at the university office of the medical investigator. She got a copy of the autopsy report. There was placental tissue in her uterus. Stella wasn't that old. It ain't over til it's over."

"'Oh what a tangled web we weave when first we practice to deceive.'" I mumbled. Note to call my inspector.

Faye's head whipped around. "What?"

"Nothing…some Sir Walter Scott." I said.

Faye glared at me. I felt a chill.

TWENTY-SIX

"Stella was pregnant," I announced as I cut the chicken enchilada casserole into large squares. God forbid anyone had to cut out his own square. I stood at the end of the kitchen table and filled each of the passed plates. I took the salad out of the refrigerator with the separate bowl of sliced tomatoes and put them in the middle of the table. I pulled garlic toast from the oven and put one slice on each plate. I sat down. Oh… tea, milk. Where was my mind? I jumped up, violently and noisily cracked ice out of prehistoric trays (I was probably the only middle-class woman in America who still had ice trays), threw some in two glasses, filled them with sun tea that I had so thoughtfully set outside in the morning, poured two glasses of milk, and slammed them down on the table sloshing liquid over the sides.

"What the--? What's wrong with you?" my husband asked.

I started shoving food in my mouth. It tasted like straw. I did not feel like talking or eating.

Max glopped spoonfuls of sour cream over his enchiladas. "Unprotected sex. Sad. Stella was old enough to know better."

"I am so sick of this entire murder!" my husband exclaimed. He slammed his fork down on the table. He spoke to the ceiling as if invoking heavenly intervention. "I don't even care anymore. My wife has turned into a Miss Marple with an attitude! She's moping around, daydreaming, distracted, working again at that dead end job, and reading romantic trash." He turned to me. " And, quite honestly, I miss my old Caroline."

"How sweet. I melt. You've always know how to talk to me," I sneered.

Douglas looked at us. Max stuffed his face. I stood up.

"I want to find the murderer! I am helping! I care! I am useful!" I exclaimed.

"Come down off your cross," John yelled. "You're still a suspect, and you know it. You're trying to save your own ass."

"Language!" Max said.

"How dare you!" I exclaimed. "Hear that kids? Your own father doesn't trust me! He took my virginity and the best years of my life! I bore his children and breastfed them."

"Too much information, Mom," Max muttered.

"Where were you that Friday night?" John pushed on.

Douglas put his fork down and started folding his napkin into a little square. Max held his fork suspended in mid air.

"You asshole! I told you! While you were passed out in your fucking Finnish chair, I was watching *Pride and Prejudice*."

"My virgin ears," Max said.

"So you say," John replied and stood up. "I've got to see a man about a horse."

"Oh! I can't stand this house!" I started to run out of the kitchen.

Douglas reached the door before me. "Mom, I have to say that I saw you driving west on Lomas that Friday night three weeks ago around 10 o'clock."

"What?"

"I was coming back from a gig at UNM Johnson Field for the Jazz Festival. The Music Department invited the top high school bands to play."

Pause. I leaned against the wall.

"Oh THAT trip down Lomas. OK. I went out for cigarettes."

"Smoking will kill you," Max said as he munched his garlic toast.

TWENTY-SEVEN

I thought I was having a heart attack. I had not had such a bad anxiety attack since my twenties when I was in the grocery store pushing a cart with one child in the kiddy seat, one child in the lower level, and a baby strapped to my chest in a Snugglie. I was shopping for the dinner I planned that night for my father and his new girlfriend. I was looking in the dairy case for yogurt. The fluorescent lights were flickering. I froze. Panic ran through my body like an electric volt. I thought I was going to faint and land on my baby. Who will take care of my children? My pounding heart! My light head! My weak body. Oh I'll die, I thought. But all I did was roll the cart to the door, pull children out, and leave the groceries. I threw the boys into the car (pre-car seat era!), drove home, collapsed on the floor on my back and tried to do a yoga exercise sending a yellow glow up my body. I eventually got bored and started some beans and chili.

But now I walked, almost ran, to Hidden Park. I entered another world through an alley camouflaged by twisting vines, cascading climbing flowers, and low leafy tree boughs. It was my Narnia. I started walking around and around on the dirt path.

I had to admit finally that I was truly a suspect. I had to wrap this entire investigation up. James was certainly dragging his feet. I could not live like this any longer. I felt heavy and scared. The walls were closing in. In my own house, no less. I don't deserve this suspicion. I hated my husband. Self-righteous butt. Years ago I was unjustly accused of having another man's child! Me! I had not had sex with anyone but my husband ever! He and his entire snooty family did not think our first son was his! I knew they were wrong, but I could do nothing! Now I felt the same helpless, smothering, panic I had during those days after Peter's birth. John and I were typed A negative blood. Baby Peter had A Positive. How did that happen? One in ten million chances, that's how. So I sweated and cried in my hospital bed. My mother held my hand. My Buddhist sister brought me *As a Man Thinketh* ("Read this and think on good things," she said softly in my ear). My mother-in-law exclaimed: "He doesn't look like a Steele baby." I didn't know what to do. Unjust! Cruel! Unusual! Torture! Immaculate Conception? Why me? And I had tried to be a good girl all my life. My mother insisted. I burst into tears when the pediatrician came in to check Peter out before I took him home. "How could my son have A Positive blood when my husband and I are A Negative?" I sobbed.

"I don't think so," the doctor said as he flipped through my chart. "John has A Positive blood. You both had your blood tested at this hospital before you were married." He turned the results so I could read them.

The truth came out. John was typed wrong in the Navy. He had to get new dog tags! But I will never forget how he and his family distrusted me. Here we go again. But not for long, I vowed. I will prevail! I stopped gnashing my teeth and muttering to myself to watch a couple kissing on a blanket. Made me think of someone.

TWENTY-EIGHT

I went to the Observatory Friday night. Late. Only three cars were in the parking lot. No telescopes set outside, no crowds, only moonlight lit my way to the closed door. But the red lights were on over the sign: If the Red Lights are On and the Door is Open, Please Come Inside. Well, don't mind if I do, I thought as I swung the unlocked door open and marched in. I saw two students chatting away standing at the entryway to the staircase leading up the huge telescope. They looked at me and then resumed their conversation. I was getting to look old enough to be invisible, I guessed. What if I wanted to see a spectacular supernova or some other heavenly something? Note to tell the Chair that they needed more welcoming helpers at the Observatory!

I felt an arm around my waist. I looked down to see Hank Burns.

"Well, if it isn't Marian the Librarian," he purred. "Stargazing or detecting?"

I tried to step back, but Hank grabbed my arm and pulled me behind one of the telescope domes in the inner courtyard.

"You're hurting me!" I said loudly hoping the grad students could hear me. But they were still laughing at each other's twerpy jokes.

"I saw the Inspector walk in. I knew you would not be far behind. Does John know about your little infatuation?"

"It's business. What you doing here?"

"I'm an astronomer, in case you've forgotten. This is an observatory. Get the connection?"

"Looking at the universe or looking for evidence, Professor?"

"I don't know what you're doing, what you're thinking, or what is going on in your menopausal head, but you are sticking your nose into matters that do not concern you."

"I'm not menopausal!"

"You are talking to the Inspector about me, I know!"

"Don't flatter yourself! I don't care about you."

"Well, you better. You don't want to get on my bad side."

"Been there done that, Frank."

Hank twisted my arm. "Bitch! You know nothing about Stella. Or me! I have to make it very clear to you what she put me through. She almost ruined my career, my tenure track position at State, and my marriage. When I heard you talk at the Martini Grill that Stella believed in the "soul" of the universe and such shit, I wanted to throw my drink in your face."

"That my husband paid for, by the way!"

"Shut up. Stella could not know soul if it hit her in the face. She did not have one. She's rotting in Hell now."

"Inspector Hutchinson knows about you," I snarled. "Snooping around the Reading Room, your competition with Stella for a position at Alma Observatory, the La Posada room card!"

"I only screwed her to find out what she proposed to Alma!" I was in a vice grip.

"Did you achieve total heavenly bliss?" I stomped on his puny foot.

Hank cursed and let me go. I ran out from behind the dome.

"Anything I can help you with, Ma'am?" Finally a young man with a nametag saw me.

"No thanks, Albert! I'll just hang out a while with the cosmos."

"Be our guest!"

I leaned against the wall closest to the students. I was shaking all over. I did deep breathing. I did not see Hank come out from behind the dome. Hiding out like the worm he was. The green door to the computer room was ajar. Faint light glowed from the screens. Shadows flickered on the north cinderblock wall. I heard low voices. I opened the door slowly and walked in. There was my Inspector talking to the Zen Master. Now I felt safe.

"If it isn't Miz Somebody!" The bearded man boomed and raised his beret in greeting revealing a three-strand comb over. Gee, he owns a comb, I thought.

"Mrs. Steele…What a pleasant surprise," Inspector James said. He wore a flight jacket. Was he a pilot, too? What a specimen!

"Oh I'm sure!" I snarked and got hot all over.

"I really mean it," James said.

"I have information to share with you. You probably already know it, but I will tell you privately. And I need to talk to you about Hank Burns." I said.

"Well, pardon me!" The Zen master exclaimed.

"No offende!"   I did not want to hurt his feelings. "It's personal."

"I'll be right back," James said to me.

James put his arm around the old man's shoulders and started walking him toward the door. Faye's tiny figure blocked the exit. Hands on each side of the doorframe.

"Faye!" James and I exclaimed.

"Wow!" said the Master.

"I want to know what's going on!" Faye exclaimed.

"Why don't you come inside and sit down," James said.

Faye walked in. Her tennis shoes were untied. She had on mismatched lacy socks. She had on plaid flannel sleepy pants and a pink tee shirt with sequined Art Saves Lives on the front. No barrette in her wild curls. She collapsed in a chair around a big table.

"Is this where she died?" she asked in a dreamy voice.

"Will someone get water?" James called out the door to the two attendants shooting the breeze.

Faye got up out of her chair, crawled up on the table, and curled up in the fetal position. I went over to her. I rubbed her back. I took her hand in mine. She stared. A student ran in with a bottle of water.

"I think her dog died," I said to James.

"On this table? Radical," the old man murmured.

Faye sat up. "Not my dog! Stella!" She screamed. "She called me here that night! She had to tell me something--wanted to make amends--to apologize to those she had wronged. She had chocolates. All friendly at first. Like an asp!" Faye started to cry. I fumbled in my purse for a Kleenex to give her. "Stella had a party going on when I got here. Her fat son, Hank Burns, sweet Cecilia--"

Just then Cecilia DeBlasi charged through the green door with such force that it banged into the wall. "Are you talking about me, you bitch? You and you (pointing a finger at me!) don't deserve to mention Stella's name!" She wore the skintight red dress, full make-up, fishnet hose, and stiletto heels. Everyone stared.

"Another audition, Cecilia?" I deadpanned.

"No! Rehearsal for *A Dolls' House*!" she sneered. "And you can call me by my stage name, Sasha Fierce!

"Oh, you and Beyoncé. Let's hear it for falsies and Spanx," I sneered back. She ran at me but stumbled when the heel of her shoe broke off. Sasha picked up the red patent leather spike, limped over to a chair, plopped down, and started to cry. "I love these."

"This must be a very modern version of Ibsen's play," The Zen Master said.

"The Dolls are an all male performing group in town who dress up like women. It's probably Dolls' house plural possessive instead of Doll's house singular possessive." (Me sounding all middle-school English teacher.) "A spoof," I clarified like a Miss Priss and Miss Prim.

Suddenly I needed clarity!

"What are you doing in an all-male revue, Cecilia?" I asked.

"Because I am sweet Cecil Deblasi, that's why!" He yanked off his wig.

Pregnant pause.

"This gives new meaning to wonders of the universe! What a show!" the Zen Master exclaimed.

James's lips twitched. He was trying not to smile. He blew his nose into a handkerchief. He cleared his throat, turned to me, and croaked: "Why is Ce...uh Sasha here?"

"I don't know! I didn't tell her about the Zen Master!" I said.

"I did!" Faye shouted. "I knew she was the one he saw running out of the green door! I told her that the truth will come out!"

Sasha jabbed the broken heel in the air. "Stella told me that she didn't love me. She loved another for years and had just lost his baby. Stella said she was sorry for leading me on. A baby! God! She used me! To do her mind numbing research, join her in sublime lovemaking…. I wrote her press releases, graded her papers, made her lesson plans, washed and ironed her costumes, combed her wigs, and then she didn't pass me on my comps! Then she found a loophole! And I passed! Thank you all over myself, Stella!!! My guardian angel! I loved her. I understood her. She couldn't help the way she was raised! She understood my gender confusion! I even sang her a song aca-pella when I got here: *Learning How to Fly.* I thought it was appropriate! I bought perfume! Knowing because she knew! I bought champagne! She laughed at me. That hurt. But when I found out that night that she never loved me, I ran out of the observatory with the champagne. I could have killed her, but I didn't."

"Hmmmmm...But the runner had overalls on as I recall," the Master spoke up.

"I did not dress for the gathering!" Sasha huffed.

"Why are you Cecilia instead of Cecil at the University?" James asked.

"I enjoy being a girl. Started hormone treatments. My voice is changing."

"I'll say," I mumbled remembering her screeching funeral solo.

"Anything wrong with that?" Sasha demanded.

"Not one bit," James answered.

"I don't care," I said.

Faye jumped to her feet. "After Ce...Sa whoever ran out, Stella told me that she continued her affair with my husband after we moved from Las Cruces to Albuquerque. She con-ceived his child. Oh did she ever rub that in. I was humiliated. Then her son yelled that he pitied any poor little bastard she brought into the world. Stella slapped him. He slapped her back. Then I slapped her. She laughed at me. 'I'm so sorry,' she purred. I wanted to kill her, but I didn't."

"And what did she tell Hank Burns?" James asked.

Faye took a deep breath. "She said that she was sorry that she plagiarized an article he wrote on building a Very Large Array on the moon. It didn't do her any good since she wasn't chosen to study at the Alma Observatory in Chile. But she wanted him to hire her as a full professor at New Mexico State. If he did not, she would tell his wife about their affair last year. He scoffed at her. Said his wife would never believe he'd risk losing his family over such an ugly, stupid woman. She told him that she had proof. Burns pressed her. She laughed. 'You loved tying me up,' she jeered. Called him the Alien Ninja. Burns shut up. He calmly walked out the door. I followed him."

James broke a long silence. "I'll need a formal statement from you all tomorrow at police headquarters. I am very upset that I did not know this information from the very beginning of this investigation."

We left the green room. The graduate student attendants were waiting impatiently to lock up. James thanked them for their extra time. We walked to the parking lot. The red lights went off. Faye hugged me before she got in her car. I kissed her. Sasha hobbled toward his car without a backward glance, still cradling the cracked heel like a wounded puppy.

The Zen Master looked up at the stars. He intoned: "There are more things in Heaven and Earth, Horatio, than are dreamed of in your philosophy." He shambled slowly down the hill. I looked at James. He was looking at the stars.

"Hamlet," he said. "Never did what he was supposed to do."

Silence. I never knew what I was supposed to do either.

"Well! So much for making amends," I blurted. "Why did Stella call this meeting?"

"A mystery. She made many people miserable. Maybe she truly wanted to make amends. But it backfired."

"Maybe her emotions were out of whack after the miscarriage. She lost a baby two weeks before she was murdered."

"I know, Mrs. Steele."

Silence.

"Are you going to interview the son?" I asked.

"Of course. And Hank Burns."

"He was very rude to me tonight. He squeezed my arm and---"

"He was here? He hurt you?" James cut in.

"Not really. He told me to stop getting involved with Stella's murder and you, actually, and---"

"He thought you and I were involved?"

"Silly, huh? He's paranoid. Had to hear all about Stella. How horrible she was. Same old story."

"Hmm." James took out his notebook and pen. He started writing.

I looked at him. His hair shone in the starlight. He put his notebook back in his pocket.

"What's with the flight jacket?" I asked as I touched the soft leather.

"Why are you here, Mrs. Steele?" he asked and covered my hand with his.

TWENTY-NINE

"Yeah, why are you here, Mom?" I was rudely knocked out of my delicious reverie to see Max. I jumped away from my Inspector.

"What are you doing here, more like it!" I exclaimed. James looked on with a little smile.

"Mom! I told you last week! My church youth group is having an overnight inter denominational prayer-a-thon for world peace at the Newman Center!"

"Then why aren't you there?"

"Oh I thought I'd get some fresh air, walk a few blocks up-hill, look at the stars, communicate with the Creator of the Universe. You know. Stuff. I saw your car, and the Observatory red lights were on so it was still open to the public."

"Where are your chaperones?"

"In the basement with Father Ignatius. I picked fresh mint in the church garden for their *mojitos.*"

"What's the Newman Center?" James asked.

"It's the Roman Catholic Community Center at the University. It's just down two blocks from here…kind of north of the Alumni Chapel where Stella had her funeral...." I started babbling and waving my hands.

"It's a very holy place," Max piped up.

"I'm sure you think so!" I replied and moved toward him. I tried to check his eyes in the dim streetlights from Lomas.

"Are those hickeys on your neck?" I demanded.

"And you are?" Max asked looking past me to the bemused James.

James came forward and extended his hand. "Hi, I'm Inspector Hutchinson." Max shook it firmly with a charming smile. Oh he will do me in yet!

"I am so sorry!" I sputtered. "Inspector Hutchinson, this is my son, Max." I glared at Max. "We are here doing some important investigating!"

James said, "So the red lights are still on? I thought the students locked up." We all looked toward the Observatory. The red lights were indeed on. "I could swear they were off when we left." Honestly, I was so looking forward to being alone with James in the parking lot that I could not recall. And my ears were ringing.

"I'm going to see if the door is unlocked," James said.

"I'll join you," Max stoutly offered.

"Please stay here, Max!" I yelled. "Let the professional handle this!"

Max started to follow the Inspector. He never listened to me! I ran to him and grabbed his arm with a motherly claw. "No! I said no!"

"Mom! I'm going!" He gently pried my hand off, and gave me a hug. "Don't worry." He turned away from me. My handsome, tall, willful son. Don't worry. Ha! All I've ever done is worry about him. "Where's Max?" was a constant question ever since he wandered away from my sister on a fishing trip in Chama when he was nine years old. We called the police and the Department of Game and Fish. Neighbors rode all-terrain vehicles over the area. I was hysterical. We had just buried my brother. I was going to lose someone else I loved. The authorities were going to bring in search and rescue dogs from Espanola at sundown. Seven hours later the phone rang. It was the Chama Police. Someone in Tierra Amarilla, a small town 15 miles away, reported that a little boy knocked on their door wearing camouflage gear. They didn't speak English. He didn't speak Spanish. But thank God the elderly couple called the police and heard of the missing child. We met on the main highway at the turn off to our cabin. I fell to my knees, clasped Max to me while I sobbed, thanking and blessing his rescuers in babbled, broken high school Spanish. The man and wife smiled.

I've never gotten over that. I thought he was dead. In the back of my mind, I'm always afraid of losing him, and he's never where he's supposed to be!

I watched Max and James as they walked up to the door, turned the handle, and entered the Observatory. I started shaking with fear for Max's safety, and then, perversely, started worrying about why the Inspector wanted to know why I was there. And he touched my hand! My life! Why am I in this situation? Why did I make the choices I've made? Why can't I be normal?

I waited. Max came out. "What's going on?" I shouted. He gave me a thumbs up, looked at the red lights and went back in.

The red lights went out. "Max! Did you fuck with the lights?" I screeched.

"Language!" came a voice. I squinted and saw a shadow sitting on the curb around the parking lot. I pulled out my IPhone, punched my handy flashlight app, and approached her. She was a young girl in a parochial school uniform and saddle shoes. Her ponytail revealed a neck decorated with a few hickeys. She covered her eyes from the thin searing beam of light.

"Aren't you supposed to be praying?" I asked dryly and turned off the app. She shrugged, pulled out a pack of Marlboro Reds from her purse and lit up. Oh! The young, the young, I thought! No shame! I looked down at her with a disapproving, hypocritical gaze.

"Call 911 now!" James shouted from the Observatory door. He came out with Max's long body slung over his shoulder!

THIRTY

"My baby!" I wailed. I rushed to them. Max's head was covered in blood. His eyes were closed.

"Max!" the girl cried. She threw her arms around his dangling legs almost knocking the Inspector over.

"Is he dead?" we both screamed.

"NO! Call 911 NOW! One of you!" James shouted almost staggering with Max's length and breadth. I fumbled with my cell. I dropped it. I was crying so hard. Miss Pony Tail whipped out her phone and coolly punched in the numbers. I suddenly got practical, ran to my car, and pulled out the blanket I used to cover the seats when my dog rode with me. Oh where is a soft surface? Only pavement! I placed it on the ground. James gently lowered Max down and removed his jacket to put under his bloody head. I took one of Max's hands and the girl took another. He had a pulse, thank God. Oh my precious one! My boy with the (natural) light in his eyes!

"What happened?" I asked James as the ambulance pulled into the parking lot. Thank goodness the University Hospital was just two blocks away. The siren muffled James's reply.

"What happened?" I cried over and over again. James grabbed my arms, put his face close to mine, "Hit on the head!" Oh my God! "I have to call his father," I said as I pulled away from his strong grip.

THIRTY-ONE

James drove little missy thing and me to the hospital. Shawna (James got her name!) refused to leave Max's side. James had contacted the campus police to report the assault. The police locked up the observatory. I called the youth group chaperones. The Calkins were indeed at the Newman Center doing god knows what but were very upset about Max. I said Shawna was with us, and I would make sure that she got home safely. The Calkins put all of us on the prayer-a-thon list.

We were silent following the ambulance. I could not speak. I could not imagine losing Max. I thought my bad luck was over. Life! I was consumed with catastrophic imaginings: Max will die. The worst. He could be blind or deaf or dumb or all three! Part of his brain could be destroyed! Like having a lobotomy! He would drool and smile all the time. Oh his spirit will be gone forever! He will have to ride the short bus to school. What if he was paralyzed from the neck down and could only move his little finger to operate his wheelchair! He could have amnesia! He could be in a coma! For years! On life support! I will read to him everyday and tell him family news. I've heard coma patients still understand. I will be there for him! I swear I will! I started hyperventilating. Shawna put her arm around me.

I was being punished for some reason! It was all about me after all. I had not been a good girl in my heart. Oh crap. Did God really care about my adulterous musings?

James dropped us off at the emergency room entrance and parked the car. John was already there. I ran into his arms and burst into tears against his broad chest. John reached for Shawna. She put her head on his chest, too. There was room. We made quite a threesome.

"He's being examined," John said. "I don't know anything else. So what the hell happened?" He looked down at Shawna. "And you are?"

"Shawna and Max took a break from the youth group at the Newman Center to walk to the Observatory. They saw my car," I started to explain.

"And what were YOU doing there? I thought you went to Target!" he demanded of me.

"I was investigating. I'll explain everything!"

"Oh God!" John threw up his hands.

James walked through the door. His flight jacket was splattered with blood. I made introductions. He suggested that we all sit down.

"Max and I were looking for the red light control box and used our cell phones for light. Max went into the Green Room. I followed him to see if he checked the inner courtyard. He wasn't in there. I saw the opened Green Room back door. I heard a scuffle, a shout, and rushed in. Max was on the floor. He did not respond to me. I had to get him out of there."

"Did you see or hear anyone?" my husband asked.

"It was pitch black. The assailant could have been up the spiral staircase or sitting on top of the telescope for all I know."

I squeezed John's hand. Who tried to kill our darling loose cannon child? And why?

A doctor walked up to us. He looked like he was in middle school.

"Mr. and Mrs. Steele?" John and I stood up. He shook our hands "I'm Dr. Stark. Your son received a nasty blow to the head. He has a concussion, but all of his vital signs are stable. He's conscious now but needs to rest. We're going to keep him overnight for observation."

"Thank goodness," I whispered. I lost all strength in my legs. I clung to John.

The doctor noticed my near collapse and quickly added, "He's going to be fine. Don't worry!"

John said, "Can we see him?"

"Only briefly and only family."

"She's his cousin," I pointed to Shawna.

Inspector Hutchinson said, "I am glad to hear this. Good to meet you John and Shawna." He shook their hands. "I'll want to talk to Max soon, however. And you, too, Mrs. Steele." James turned and left the emergency room.

John gave me a brief look but quickly made his way into the examination room. Shawna and I followed. John just stood there looking at his son with silent tears running down his cheeks. I took Max's hand and kissed it. Shawna kissed him on his cheek. Max's droopy eyes opened. He gave a weak smile and a thumbs up.

The next morning I woke up around 7 AM alone in bed. I finally fell asleep around 3 AM. I started crying remembering last night's traumatic events and what could have been. Oh be thankful, I said out loud, and went into the kitchen. A note was on the counter from John. He was visiting Max before going to a meeting at the IRS. He would be back at the hospital around noon. Fine, I thought, as I gratefully poured a cup of my CPA's delicious coffee.

THIRTY-TWO

"Mom! You will not believe it! I was attacked by a wild person! He looked like Bob in Twin Peaks! You know the one? The freak who climbed up the walls of Laura's house to peek in the windows! With the long greasy hair? You remember?" Max stopped his exclamations to shovel scrambled eggs covered in catsup into his mouth. His tray was filled with juice, Cheerios, bacon, milk, and French toast. I thought people were nauseated after concussions.

"Max…please don't get too excited," I murmured.

I stood on one side of his bed. Shawna stood on the other side. The Inspector sat in a chair taking notes. Brother Douglas sat in another chair pretending to read *The Wind Up Bird Chronicle*. "Bob was one strange character," Douglas mused lowering his book. "I love David Lynch."

"I can't believe I let you boys watch those videos," I said.

Douglas said, "Remember when I broke my leg, had to stay home from school and we had a David Lynch movie marathon?"

"Oh! Well, it was fun…and artistic, but I must have been in a liberal state of mind." I noticed the Inspector was writing something down. Probably "twisted mother" or something.

Shawna said, "I love *Wild at Heart*."

"Wasn't that X rated?" I asked. Shawna shrugged.

"My favorite is *Mulholland Drive*," James said.

"I've watched that three times and still don't understand what went on!" I said all animated.

"I'll tell you what I think…" he said then stopped. "Another time."

"Excuse me for interrupting your film group!" Max said. "I'm trying to tell you what happened! A crime has been committed upon my person!"

"Let's continue, Max. You need to rest," James said.

"So I walked into the back of the Observatory through the rear Green Room door. Used the cell phone glow. I heard someone moving around. I said 'hello' but no answer. I found the staircase and looked under it. My light shone on what I can only say was a long, stringy haired, disembodied head. It rose up, turned, and hit me with something."

"Can you describe the face?" James asked as he scribbled away.

"Just saw bared teeth," Max replied.

THIRTY-THREE

Max came home that day. I called his school Monday to say he would be out all week. I called Faye to tell her I could not be in that week. She had already heard what happened. The department sent Max a get-well card signed by mostly everyone. Even Griselda printed her name with a feathery drawn heart underneath. Max had many visitors and well wishers who brought books, candy, stuffed teddy bears, and DVDs. Shawna walked over from Our Lady of Fatima School every day to sit by his side. The St. Mark's Youth Group sent balloons and prayer cards. I bustled around making his favorite foods. Douglas picked up Max's homework from his teachers everyday and returned the completed assignments. Max fell asleep to the sound of John playing his Celtic harp. Peter called him every morning from Austin. I have a very caring family, I realized.

My Inspector came by once to check on Max. I was all hospitality offering tea and freshly baked Ghirardelli chocolate chip cookies with walnuts. James did not ask me any questions about the case. I was relieved. We talked about New Orleans.

He complimented my home and liked my dog. Suki liked him, too. I walked him out to his car, a light green VW Passat.

"So you do have a car! I love Volkswagens," I said and waved at my cute beetle parked in the driveway.

"Yes, I finally had to get one. Albuquerque buses did not run on my schedule," James said as he put his key in the door. Then he stopped. "The Zen Master came to headquarters yesterday."

"Oh?"

"Yes. He wanted to tell me that he recognized a silver beetle that was in the parking lot the night Max was injured. He remembered that one was parked there the night Stella was killed."

"Oh? Well, a lot of people drive those beetles!" I said. I felt dizzy. He stared at me. "Don't they?" I asked.

"Of course they do, Mrs. Steele." He got in his car and rolled down the window. "I like your cookies." I had a hot flash.

My husband and I did not discuss my involvement with the murder mystery. We were so thankful to have our son alive and well. But the subject was like the elephant under the table. We were friendly. The house was peaceful. One night, after a few glasses of wine, I thought I was strong enough. I hauled *The Love Crescent* out from under my bed. I read:

Pilar and Jesse rode out to the dastardly dude's hacienda. Jesse had his long barrel shotgun and six-shooter. Pilar tucked her silver derringer snugly in red velvet ribbon garter that she always wore high on her smooth, well-toned, wild dark honey hued right thigh. They rode like the wind on the pounding hooves of their noble steeds. Nearing the property they were greeted by barking dogs. Pilar jumped off her horse and walked up to the snarling, frenzied pack. She bent over their snappy jaws and looked them in the eye. The dogs rolled over onto their backs. She rubbed their tummies gently. They whined.

"Oh my own dog whisperer," Jesse whispered. "You witch!" He dismounted. He walked over to Pilar, lifted the fringed border of her buckskin skirt and kissed it. The dogs whined.

(Oh now she glamours like a vampire, I huffed. Note to tell Tina that she is mixing her genres!)

"Oh you!" Pilar gushed. The dogs whined. Jesse pulled some buffalo jerky out of his saddlebag and threw it to the dogs. They hunkered down for a long chew.

Jess and Pilar tied their horses to a tree. Jessie gave them each an apple out of his saddlebag.

"You are so kind to animals," Pilar said in a throaty voice.

"They are God's creatures," Jesse replied reverently.

Pilar responded non-verbally by giving him a deep kiss. He gently squeezed her ripe breast that peeked out over her buckskin vest.

"Don't stop," she moaned.

"We must do what we came to do." He lifted his flexible thumb off her nipple.

"My man," Pilar said.

Then they crept stealthily up to the adobe house.

"You go left. I'll take the right," Jesse said forcefully.

Looking in the windows they both saw two men playing cards. They were drinking whiskey out of a bottle and smoking cigars. Their guns were on the table along with a chicken carcass and a plate of corn bread crumbs. They were laughing and cussing out one another.

Pilar saw Jesse jerk his head toward the front door. She crept around to meet him. He kicked the door opened. The two men inside dropped their jaws. One had broken, jagged green teeth. The other had no teeth. As they reached for their weapons, Jesse shot the guns right off the table.

"You're alive!" The outlaws said in unison when they saw Pilar.

"You bet your ass I'm alive," she shouted. I am here to avenge the deaths of my family and pets!" She whipped out her derringer.

"Hot damn! If it ain't Annie Oakley! You need a bigger gun, Sister Sue!" The one-eyed man sneered.

Pilar delivered a stinging slap to his face.

"That hurt, little missy, but not as much as this will." Quick as lightening he grabbed Pilar, reached behind to pull out the Bowie knife hanging off the back of his belt and pointed it at her throat. "Now back off, knight in shining armor or whoever you are! Or I'll scalp this little minx before your eyes!"

Jesse dropped his rifle and pistol. "Don't hurt her, please! She's been through so much."

"Oh, yeah? What has she told you anyway, pilgrim? Poor little orphan, huh? Bathed in blood? Played dead to survive? Well, bull corn I say!"

"Don't believe anything he says, Jesse, my love!" Pilar choked. The knife pierced her throat. A stream of bright red blood flowed down her breasts.

"She knew she couldn't get away with it! She had the money!"

"What money?" Jesse asked.

"Then things went terribly wrong. Eustace over there was high on the peyote buttons. He went crazy...."

That's enough! I slammed the manuscript closed. Tina must have been smoking something to write this. I needed to smoke something to read this. I dumped *The Love Crescent* on the floor and turned out the light.

THIRTY-FOUR

Tina called. She wanted my responses to *The Love Crescent* so far. I waited until Shawna walked over from Our Lady of Fatima Parochial School to visit Max at 2:30. Maybe that was a mistake to leave them alone even for thirty minutes, but the best chaperone in the world, his brother Douglas, came home at 3:00. And Max still seemed weak. I thought.

I parked in front of her little adobe house with the lace curtains in the windows. I hauled out the manuscript and my typed notes. Tina greeted me so warmly. I loved this woman. And envied her. There she was resplendent in a long flowing ethnic skirt, floral sandals, an off the shoulder white peasant blouse, and naturally black, permed to the max, long curly hair. I had on jeans, a black tee shirt, and flip-flops. I had sprayed water over my bed head hair to smash it down. We walked through her lush, plush, purple velvet living room with tiny, fringed lamps and embroidered fringed pillows. A crystal chandelier hung in the middle of the ceiling. We sat in her den with colorful, gauzy fabric swooshing from one side of the walls to another. I felt like I was in a sheik's tent. We sat on tufted, lilac chairs. On a little curlicue end table was a silver tray laden with a china tea service.

Tina also had three sons. Our families grew up together. Her children were all athlete scholars. While mine, except for perfect Peter, were playing drums, getting mediocre grades, and smoking pot. She wrote all day (imagine!) while I ran around in circles. She had a handsome husband and so did I. They slept in a double bed while a king-sized mattress was not big enough for me. She diced. I chopped.

"Oh Caro! I'm so glad to see you!" she said pouring me a fragrant cup.

"Tina! It's good to see you, too."

"How are you?"

"Well," I started to tell her all about Stella's murder, why I was a suspect, and the handsome inspector. I told her about Max.

"I'm so glad he's OK! How scary! But…oh…this sounds like a novel! Have you ever thought about writing this down?"

"Someday. I am obsessed with finding the murderer. It's hard. Everyone hated her!"

"One murders for sex or money."

"Really?" My brain synapses fired immediately. Dolores and Brian needed money. Cecil/Cecilia and Hank had sex with Stella. Faye's ex-husband had sex with Stella. What a ménage a trois! My head was spinning. "Really?" I repeated.

"Really. Have a scone. With clotted cream."

I handed her my typed notes. She said she'd read them later. I was probably not the right person to respond to her bodice-ripper novel. I never read them, but Tina was already in a writer's group and wanted an outside opinion, too. She valued my thoughts, she said. I felt unworthy.

"Was Pilar's family murdered for money?

"I'll never tell!"

"I'll continue on with anticipation!" I said like any gentle responder.

"So what about this Inspector?" she asked and flicked cream off the side of her mouth with her tongue.

"He's gorgeous. I'm having all kinds of fantasies," I said and licked cream off the tips of my fingers.

"Write, girl, write! Imagination rules!" Tina spooned homemade raspberry jam on my scone.

"You have them?" I asked and took a large bite of dripping scone.

"They're my life!" She wiped a drop of jam off her cleavage with two fingers.

"So...some of *The Love Crescent* isn't based on..." I swallowed and patted my mouth with a yellow cloth napkin.

"Caro. You are an innocent flower! I see my life as a movie. Better than going to a therapist. I escape...do you ever role play?" She pushed hair out of her face with her wrist.

"Only on stage," I sighed.

"If I may quote the Bard: 'All the world's a stage. And all the men and women merely players,'" Tina started.

"They have their exits and their entrances," I finished. "And one man in his time plays many parts."

"And one woman plays many parts, too, for her own good!" Tina said. "Do I have jam in my hair?"

THIRTY-FIVE

I drove home buzzing on a sugar high. Sex or money, huh? Well, well. This was food for thought, indeed! Thinking of food, I had to make something for dinner. Something savory… salty…cheesy…a little crunch. God knows nothing sweet! I'll make a bacon quiche. But real men don't eat quiche. They'll eat it and like it, I thought, as I pulled into the driveway.

I felt very energetic as I threw some bacon in a pan, measured flour into a bowl, plopped some Crisco, salt, and ice water on top, and cut it into pebble sized balls with two knives. Suki clacked around me in circles as she sensed my excitement. Who killed Stella because of sex? Was it that good? Or that bad? I thought only Cecilia really loved her. Burns wanted information. And Stella was blackmailing him. I tossed the knives into the sink with a crash. Suki ran out of the kitchen. I turned over the bacon. I dove into the flour mixture with both hands squishing and molding it into a ball. I sprinkled flour on the counter top and all over my rolling pin. Suki slunk back in the kitchen and sat at my feet. Ever hopeful. I placed the sticky ball on the counter, got a handful of flour and threw it all over the wad.   And everywhere else.   Some landed on Suki's head. She started sneezing violently. Hank hated Stella! I brushed off Suki's snout with a dishtowel. She ran under the kitchen table with her ears flattened. Sorry, girl! Where was I? Oh…Faye's husband may have loved Stella, or was she just a casual affair? But she did get pregnant by him, and Faye never could. And Stella told Faye! I started rolling the blob into a circle. Faye hated Stella! And money! Dolores needed money! Her mother was driving her crazier than usual. The bacon was crisp. I drained it on some paper towels. I pinched off some fatty ends, blew on them, and bent over to feed them to Suki. Her ears perked up. Dolores had to put her mother in care! I resumed rolling. But how could Dolores get money from Stella? The dough stuck to my rolling pin. Was she blackmailing her? How? Saw her buggering a grad student?   Pulled accounting strings to reward Stella's projects? I peeled the dough off and threw more flour on it. And Brian! He needed to be on his own! No help from his mother. And no help in the future, he thought. Another betrayal; another abandonment in his eyes. How could she do this to him? Again! And his mother was pregnant! Another child coming into the world for her to torture! Or maybe he believed this child would be treasured. Not like him! I rolled out a shape that resembled the state of Alaska and surrounding islands. Brian hated his mother! I scraped Alaska off the counter with a spatula. I mashed the dough artistically into a pie plate. I grated cheese, whipped up eggs and cream, crumbled the bacon, and poured the viscous lumpy mixture on top of the crust.

"Mom! Looks like there was a snow storm in here!" Max exclaimed as he walked in the kitchen. "What are you doing?"

"I'm thinking," I said as I wrapped my arms around him. We burst into laughter as I stepped away. He was covered in flour like me.

THIRTY-SIX

Max went back to school. Or at least that's where I thought he went during the day. Back to a normal, familiar worry. I returned to work. I looked suspiciously at Dolores's long, stringy gray hair. Was it greasy or just plain dirty? Was there a difference? I wondered how some strands got clumped together. Product? I thought not! I tore my eyes away from her scalp when she asked about Max. Griselda bustled into the reading room helping me dust, always asking about the *pobrecito Niño*. She had crocheted him a stocking cap with purple, orange, and red stripes. "For his cabeza! Will protect him always!" Faye was subdued, but I was relieved to see a barrette firmly in place. Cecil/Cecilia loped around in coveralls and talked to Hal at length about the Hawaiian doctoral fellowship. I looked suspiciously at Yvonne's long, black banana curls. I looked suspiciously at Lorraine's scarecrow hair.

Stella's son had long, dirty hair. But Faye said that he had left town with his grandparents. He could have come back.

Hank Burns, the little fucker, had perfectly combed and parted *Father Knows Best* short hair.

I hoped for some word from my inspector. What was he doing? What did he know? I needed to do something even if it was wrong. I left the Reading Room.

I asked Faye if I could see Stella's office. She nodded and pulled out her keys from her Hello Kitty purse. I followed her tiny, tightly wound body down the hall. I wanted to say something, but words failed me. Faye tried so hard. Too hard. But I was not in her moccasins. Who knows what I would be without my husband, children, and dog: A free spirit living near the ocean with a dog and teaching English at a school where everyone was nice? Acting in a small, rustic community theatre where no one was bitchy? Only a dream I had.

But I had to get down to the reality of the situation. I turned on the office light. The costumes were still hanging eerily on the rack. Someone should call the Theatre Department! Maybe Cecil/Cecilia wants them. I went through all the empty drawers. Looked under the desk. Looked under the blinds on the windowsills. The bookshelves had a few dusty catalogs. The bulletin board blank. I flipped through the cat calendar on the wall. I started taking every item of clothing off the hangars and throwing them on the floor. They reeked of Knowing perfume. Stella's smell. Still gave me the creeps. Knowing. What did Stella know? I opened a window for fresh air.

I sat down next to the crumpled heap of Star Trek costumes. I separated the girls from the boys. Hard to tell, but they had official Trekkie identity badges on the chest. Some had darts ripped out to accommodate Stella's huge cleavage. Now Deanna Troi's were very feminine with beautifully colored horizontal magenta stripes. I fluffed it out. Turned it around and around and inside out. In Stella's dreams could she ever pull Troi off, I harrumphed. I pulled out Lt. Uhura. Tailored, masculine, but a plunging neckline. Bet Stella loved wearing this. No pockets. Flat seams. What's this? Lt. Tasha Yar? I clasped her uniform to my chest and sighed. She was so pretty. I remembered the episode when she made love with the android Data. Lt. Yar reported later: "He's fully functional." Oh my! To be on the Enterprise with my Inspector! There I was again in fantasyland. I should write a novel or return to therapy. Or I needed to re-read *How To Love What You Have*. Later. Now I searched the seams and folds of Tasha's costume. The zipped pocket on the side of the pants crinkled. I pulled out a sheet of paper. I read tlhIngan Hol. What language was that? A code?

I called Inspector Hutchinson but got his voice mail.

"Playing dress-up, Chica?" Griselda was at the door at attention clutching her sweep broom. I ended my call without leaving a message.

"Oh yes!" I said cheerily. "I don't know why the department hasn't donated these to community theatres!"

"They stink, that's why. Stella was dirty inside and out."

"Sad, but true," I agreed slipping the paper into my jean pocket as I stood up.

"Calling someone?" Griselda asked blocking the door with her substantial body.

"Just my therapist," I sighed as I stepped over her broom into the hall.

"Chica! Have a little faith in yourself!"

"Working on it!" I closed Stella's office door, hugged Griselda, looked suspiciously at her shiny, thickly braided bun, and walked calmly down the hall. I turned the corner. Dolores ran into me wearing her gray long poufy coat, long gray hair spilling over the fake fur collar, carrying a handful of files.

"W-WHOAH! Sorry!" she said.

"Me, too!"

"In a hurry?"

"I found something in Stella's office."

"W-what?"

"Oh nothing."

"Nothing?"

"Nothing, I said."

"You're moving too f-fast for nothing. You have a red f-face."

"I was looking at costumes in there. I tried one on. I got hot."

"So you discovered what?"

"See you!" I started to walk away. Dolores moved right in front of me. Too close. Invading my personal space. Her files poked my chest.

I stepped back from her. "Dolores, really, it's nothing. A piece of paper in Lt. Yar's pocket with phone numbers. I want to rush it over to Inspector Hutchinson."

"Just phone numbers? You're sure they're phone numbers? Let me l-look at them. I might recognize some."

"I think not. The area codes are not Albuquerque 505s but thanks ever so anyway! Hey! I'll let you know what comes of this! OK?"

Dr. Winter, the Chair, walked up to us. "Dolores! Glad I caught you before you went to General Accounting. I need some paperwork for our new hire."

"I-I…" Dolores said as she turned to Dr. Winter. I walked away.

THIRTY-SEVEN

My cell rang as I started the car. My hands were shaking. My heart was pounding.   I ratcheted around in my purse and finally found my phone.

"You called?" James asked.

"I will call you back once I'm out of the parking lot," I said breathlessly.

"Where are you?"

"At work! I found something in Stella's office!"

"Are you all right?"

"I'm confused."

"Meet me at Hidden Park."

"How do you know about--" James hung up.

There he was sitting on a bench with his legs crossed, wearing chinos, a plaid shirt, Doc Martin's, and his Ray-Bans. He got up to kick a soccer ball back to a young boy with his father. So graceful. I thought. James saw me.

"How are you?"

"I am mentally, physically, and emotionally fatigued," I said. "How's Max?"

"His normal exciting self."

"Good! Let's eat." He reached for a brown bag next to him. I stood there like a dork. He patted the bench.   He opened the sack, handed me a napkin, half a sandwich, a bunch of red grapes, and a little bag of Doritos. He took two small bottles of Perrier out of his jacket pocket.

"Is this your lunch?" I asked.

"Why, yes."

"Did you make it yourself?"

"Yes. I thought we deserved a break today."

"And I thought you were going to be out until late afternoon!"

"I was thinking."

"Oh! One must take time to think." I watched James unscrew the tops of the Perrier waters with such flare. He gave me one. We clinked. We sipped.

"Ah! Civilized. All is well for now, Mrs. Steele."

In companionable silence we shared the turkey and avocado sandwich, the grapes and chips.

"Why did you leave New Orleans?" I asked.

"It was time," James said.

"Do you have family there?"

"Yes."

"I'm sure they miss you."

Silence.

"So did you grow up there, or...."

Another ball came rolling towards us. James stood up and kicked it back to the young boy. His father waved a thank you.

"You have a strong right foot! Have you played soccer?"

"I've played and coached."

"My husband coached our son Douglas's team for a year." James put our empty plastic bags in the paper sack. "Do you have any children?"

"Why did you call me, Mrs. Steele?"

I looked at him. He looked at me. I got the hint. "Thank you for lunch," I said. I picked up the trash and walked it over to the garbage bin. I watched the father and son leave the park.

I sat back down next to him. I showed him the piece of paper.

"I found this in of one of Stella's Star Trek costumes in her office. I don't know what it means. Why did Stella have it?"

"Hmmm," James said as he took it from me. He read it over. "Good work, Mrs. Steele."

He took off his sunglasses. I took off mine. We stared at each other for a long time. Again.

"Anything else?" he finally asked.

My heart started beating fast. I flushed. I jumped up and started pacing back and forth in front of the bench waving my hands.

"I have to say it! I went to the Observatory the night of the murder! Stella called me. She said that she had a surprise for me, that she missed me, and wanted to talk about the past. I said no, but she begged me to come around nine. She had invited other people. They wanted to see me again, too! I told her maybe. I didn't want to see that woman ever again! But after John fell asleep in his chair, I started thinking about what kind of surprise she had in store for me. And, to tell the truth, I was bored--a very dangerous state for me. I make emotional decisions rather than thinking things through. I feel like I'm missing something and dive into whatever I hope might stimulate me. I often make bad choices."

"Oh do you now?" James said.

"I do! So I got in my car about 10:00. I drove down Lomas. That's when my son Douglas saw me. I got to the Observatory.

The red lights were off, but I parked my car and walked up to the outer door. It was locked. I got back in my car and drove home. Stella must have cancelled her party. Maybe no one came, I thought at the time. Gave me a sick pleasure."

"Any other cars in the parking lot?"

"No!"

"Of course faculty and staff could have parked their cars in the Physics and Astronomy Building lot a block away. And there's always the bus stop two blocks down the hill," he mused.

"I did not kill Stella."

"Please sit back down, Mrs. Steele."

I plopped down on the bench.

"What a beautiful park," James said at last.

"Yes," I said. "Why did you pick this park for our meeting?"

"I investigated, Mrs. Steele."

Birds were trilling. A gentle breeze ruffled the leaves in the trees. Classical music wafted out a nearby window. I smelled bacon. I felt bubbly.

"Well, investigate this," I said.

I flung my leg over his lap and straddled him. I looked into his green eyes. I took a handful of his beautiful hair. I bent to kiss him. He put his hands around my waist stopping me mid lunge.

"Are you bored, Mrs. Steele?" he asked.

"Stupefied," I whispered. He relaxed his hold on me. I touched his lips with mine.

"Over here! Over here! I go in first!!! No ME!!! I go in first!!!" high-pitched voices yelled.

"You ALL can go at the same time! CALM DOWN!" boomed a deep voice.

The inspector and I turned our heads, cheeks touching, and saw children racing into the park from the alley followed by a man carrying a large case. Other adults straggled in. One carried a cake. The man dumped the box on the ground, popped it open, another man knelt down and attached some device to a corner. My inspector and I watched, awe-struck, as a Big Bopper Bounce House inflated before our eyes. The kids were screaming, running, skipping, hopping, and waving their arms around the swollen monstrosity. Looked like a tribal ceremony.

We both faced each other again. Nose to nose. We burst into laughter. I uncurled myself from the inspector's lap. One of his hands stayed on my waist.

"I'm so embarrassed," I started to say all sincerely but ended up shrieking with hysterical laughter. James looked at me. He wrapped his arm around my waist. He wiped his eyes with his other hand. I threw my head back against his shoulder. I needed to blow my nose. I was a mess of tears and snot. I started to hiccup.

"I need water," I said.

"That's not all you need," James murmured. He took an aluminum water bottle out of his jacket pocket. He's so prepared.

"What?" His comment finally registered.

I took 21 quick sips of water. Relief!

"I said I need to get to work," James said clearly. We stood up. With his arm around my waist we walked out of Hidden Park. I felt weak but cleansed. I was calm, for once. I was light. The Spanish saying came to my mind: "There is no happiness, only moments of happiness."

James opened my car door for me. I got in. I rolled down the window.

"Thanks again for lunch," I said. "I don't know what…."

"Thanks for all your good Owork, Mrs. Steele." He said abruptly. I watched him walk away talking on his cell phone. Catching a bus? Who knows about him. I'll try not to know. I think.

THIRTY-EIGHT

I walked back into the Physics and Astronomy building. The office was still closed for lunch. Slackers! I needed to get back into the Reading Room, do stupid work and think about my Inspector in peace. Maybe Dolores was back from burger heaven. She'll have a key.

Her door was open. No Dolores. I'll wait. I looked at her mother's picture. Poor Dolores. Her father died when she was sixteen. Her older brother left New Mexico, got married, and has never been back. She stayed home with her mother. Now pushing 60 years old, her life has been one of academics, job, caretaking, and eating crap. And fashion don'ts.

I walked over to the Star Ship Enterprise blueprints. Like who wants to know the name of every part of a spaceship? In two languages? Delores, of course. And there were the Klingons. I remembered the sub-commander Klingon Worf and a Klingon woman making love. They pulled each other's hair and growled. I drifted into a pleasant TV memory daydream while I stood in front of this Star Ship blueprint. Who knew someone had developed an entire Klingon language? Hmmm.

Strange. But something caught my eye: tlhlngan Hol at the top of the blueprint. I pulled a copy I had made of the slip of paper I found in Lt. Yar's uniform out of my purse: tlhlngan Hol. Was this a key? A password? Why did Stella have this: a direct connection to Dolores's Klingon poster? Why was it hidden? Did Dolores use this for computer access?

"You read Klingon?" I turned around and saw Dolores in the doorway. "Need something?

I dropped the slip of paper into my opened purse. "I have to get back in the reading room."

"What's on that p-paper you were reading?"

"Oh a grocery list! Lots of mouths to feed at home! Always running out of something!"

"Harrumph," Dolores muttered and went out the door.

"Thank you, Dolores," I said following her down the hall.

I sat down in the Reading Room. My head was spinning. The walls were closing in on me. I needed a computer. Fast. I wanted to try this tlhlngan Hol word in some software. I did not want an audience. Perhaps these Klingon words were access to Dolores's accounting software. Stella may have used it to check on Dolores's financial activities. To make sure Dolores was processing her projects? Or was Stella checking up on other departmental accounts? Comparing her monies with everyone else's?

No one had moved Stella's computer out of her office yet. I hoped. I saw it in there a few days ago. I propped the door with a bite-sized Kit Kat bar from my purse and went to the bathroom. On the way out I ran into Griselda.

"Can you let me into Stella's office?" I asked.

"Bad vibes, Chica. You don't want to be in there anymore."

"Please."

"*Muy loca*," she muttered as we walked down the hall.

My heart was beating fast. But I was on a mission! I closed the door, sat down at Stella's desk, and turned on her computer. Her Han Solo screen saver came up. Harrison Ford used to be cute. I went into the UNM website, clicked on My UNM and typed in my NETID and password. I then went to Employee Life. I wanted to access some business software. I'll try Banner where all the information one has to know about students, finances, schedules, and transcripts are held. What could be Dolores's NETID? Mine was the first letters of my e-mail account. Maybe hers was, too. I typed in dblack. OK. Password. I typed in tlhlinganHol. Rejected. Of course it had to have a number in it somewhere. What's her birthday? March 26th. I typed various twenty-sixes in between all the letters. What year was she born? I tried forty-seven everywhere. This was driving me crazy. Numbers, numbers…what would she use? Her mother's birthday? What did she love besides McDonald's? Star Trek. Pussycats. The U.S.S. Enterprise going where no man has gone before? I minimized the screen and went on Google. I typed in Star Trek. Too much information! Fanatics out there! But I did find the number of the Enterprise: 1701. This will take some time, I grumbled. But a miracle happened! I typed 17 in front of tlhlinganHol and 01 after. In! Now what? Banner programs were like alphabet soup. SSPQ, AASAS, so forth and so on. How do people live with this? I started with all the As thinking, silly me, that it meant accounting. Enough of this. I went to the UNM Accounts Receivable website and went on a Banner tutorial. How does anyone do this for a living? Soul crunching labor. I found FZPDDEZ where a sample came up of money going out to a vendor. All right. My brain was squeezed. I needed fresh air and a smoke. But I chewed some gum and went back to Banner, signed in with the gobble-dygook, and scrolled through all the money reimbursed to the department for the month. All these Institutes and Centers! This department must have the major money to spend. I read an odd one: Institute for Quantum Photonics and Social Phenomenon was invoiced and got reimbursed $1,000. I stopped. I picked up the current Physics and Astronomy catalog from Stella's bookshelf. I looked up the list of Institutes and Centers. Not listed. This one must be very new.

I heard a key in the door. I minimized the screen quickly.

"Ch-checking your e-mail?" Dolores asked as she entered and slammed the door behind her.

I stood up. "Sorry to waste my time on the job! Haha! Don't want to cheat the university of any money," I said. She pushed me aside to sit in the chair in front of the computer. She hit a key and the current Banner screen came up.

"You'll have m-me to answer to if you do, you know," Dolores said as she got up and turned off the lights.

"What are you doing, Dolores?" I asked in my strong student teacher voice.

"I am doing what I h-have to do."

"What? Setting up a fake institute, invoicing the department, and pocketing the money?"

"I have to p-put her away!" she yelled. "I need the money! She's killing me! She'll outlive us all!" She came at me, hair flying, teeth bared. I stepped back and fell into the pile of costumes on the floor. Her bony body landed on top of me. She grabbed the Klingon Worf's wig and started stuffing it in my mouth. I gagged, yanked Dolores's scraggly hair, and twisted throwing her off. I spit out the long, black hairs. Dolores bounced back whacking me with a toy light saber. I went down again. I grabbed her spindly ankles. She stumbled, threw the plastic saber away, and drew out a pair of scissors tucked in her ratty belt.

"Dolores! You don't want to do this! You will not get away with it!"

She started to circle me while waving the scissor back and forth. Eerie light came from the glow-in-the-dark stars on the ceiling.

"I've already killed one person. I got away with it, too."

"You almost killed my son!" I screamed.

"Collateral damage!"

"The Inspector has the password. If anything happens to me--"

"I'll take that chance. You are not going to ruin me like h-her!"

"I don't want to ruin you, Dolores!"

"Stella did! She never b-believed me that NASA had rejected her proposals. She had a student hack into my UNM account. She f-found out about the fake institute. She was going to expose me if I didn't create a research account for her to finance her dream of working in Chile. And she wanted h-half of all the money for my mother's nursing home that I had illegally gotten from the department. I faced joblessness, n-no insurance, no retirement, fines, and a life of day and night wiping the b-butt of a rotten human being who never loved me."

"I am so sorry."

"Not so sorry! You want to expose me, too!"

"I was looking for the truth."

"I-I'll tell you the truth. I loved strangling Stella."

We continued to circle each other. I was getting dizzy. And very frightened.

Dolores sneered, "You know what tlhlngan Hol means?"

"So that's how you pronounce it. How clever!"

"Don't patronize me! It means hello and good-bye in Klingon. So good-bye."

She ran at me with raised scissors. I crouched down to the floor. She tumbled over my body and fell. Dolores struggled to get up. I crawled over to a chair and rolled it into her. Before Dolores regained her balance, I jumped up and kicked her knees. She fell down. I grabbed the arm waving the scissors She tried to bite me. I head butted her. It hurt. I put both my hands around her wrist. Her bones were so light, so frail, so thin, so like a little bird I thought as I twisted until I heard a crack. She dropped the scissors with a blood-curdling howl. I kicked them into the wall. Light flooded Stella's office. A screeching woman flew in. Dolores looked at her with horror. Griselda hit Dolores with a broom. Dolores's head hit the floor with a thud. She was out cold.

Griselda put her foot on Dolores's chest. "Chica! I told you this place had bad vibes!"

THIRTY-NINE

I drove home to a quiet house. I hugged my dog. I ate a Kit Kat while I stared out the kitchen window. I collapsed on my bed. God help me but I picked up *The Love Crescent*. Oscar Wilde said that life imitated art. Is *The Love Crescent* art? Oh I don't know anything anymore. I read:

...and started shooting everything that moved. I couldn't stop him!"

"You lie! You dastardly bastard! Oh Jesse! They were go-ing to send me back to Mexico! Not to marry a cousin! Oh no! There was a bounty out on my head! I was trafficked in the flesh trade to a Comandante Supremo! I was his sex slave! I was kidnapped from my loving family while on vacation in New Or-leans! I was only 15!"

"My poor angel," Jesse said.

"Shut yer trap, woman!" Eustace pulled Pilar's hair.

"Then the old devil tired of me! He was planning to send me to Morocco to be in a sheik's harem! Via Spain! I crawled out a window, ran to a train station, hid in a cattle car going to El Paso. I ran to a church. The good sisters reunited me with my family."

"You robbed all the money in his safe first!" lisped Eustace. The Supremo told us! Where did you hide it? We were supposed to get a cut of what you stole plus the bounty on yer head!"

"We could have gotten good money if you hadn't shot her!" snarled Uno (the one-eyed man).

"Now don't you go blaming Eustace!" yelled Eustace.

"I'm calling a spade a spade!" Uno cried as he flung Pilar against the wall and stabbed Eustace.

"Oh I die!" croaked Eustace.

"You're not the only one!" growled Jesse as he quickly snatched a greasy plate off the table, broke it and slit Uno's throat with a pottery shard.

"Jesse gently lifted a rather stunned Pilar into his strong arms. He carried her out the door and placed her gently on a grassy knoll under a tree. Pilar moaned. The dogs whined.

"My darling," she sighed.

"My own treasure," Jesse murmured. "So where is it?"

"All in good time, my sweet, all in good time," Pilar whispered.

Well, all for money, I thought. A thieving Jezebel. I slammed the manuscript shut. I will read the end later. Probably they'll ride off into the sunset with a future bright with sex and saddlebags of money until they get old, demented and bald. I should write my own ending. Heh heh.

I started to make lasagna. I was exhausted. What a day. I almost got killed, but more importantly I made a fool of myself with the Inspector. He seemed to take it well, however. It was all so ridiculous. There I was throwing myself at him. There were the children bouncing and bopping. Life! I shouldn't take it (or myself) so seriously. It was a silly place. But I was certainly glad to be here. Poor Dolores.

The phone rang. It was Faye. The Inspector wanted to meet with us tomorrow.

FORTY

I sat with Faye, Hal, Lorraine, Griselda, Yvonne, and Cecil/Cecilia in the lounge. Inspector Hutchinson entered. He flipped open a notebook then returned it to his pocket.

"Dolores Black confessed to the murder of Stella Cummings. She is being held without bond. She has a court appointed lawyer who has requested a psychiatric evaluation."

(Shocking outbursts from everyone)

"What happens to her mother?" I asked.

James reached into his pocket for his notebook. He turned some pages.

"She is in the State Hospital in Los Lunas."

"All that money Dolores siphoned off only to have her committed to the state," I said.

"The money was retrieved in full. It was in a separate bank account at the credit union under the name of a Miss Thea Hol."

"Nothing like an accountant to deposit even ill-gotten gains in a bank," Lorraine whispered.

"Under a Klingonesque name!" Faye said.

"That reminds me," James said as he pulled out a chair to sit down next to us. "We are in debt to Caroline Steele's curious nature. She found crucial incriminating evidence and almost got killed in the process. We must also acknowledge the brave action of Griselda Santamajor who saved Caro's life."

Everyone stood up and clapped!

James walked over to me. He handed me my tattered notebook. "I don't need this anymore, Mrs. Steele." This got a laugh.

Cecil/Cecilia clapped her hands and stood up. We all sat down.

"I just want to say that Stella had many good qualities. I loved her. Students loved her. She had her demons. Don't we all? But we should do no harm. May she rest in peace. That's all." She sat down.

"Amen, honey," Hal said.

FORTY-ONE

My life went on. I shopped, cooked, cleaned, and did laundry. I walked my dog. I did yoga. I read all afternoon. I went to my Reading Group once a month to discuss bleeding heart miserable literary books and drink hot water. I went to my bridge group once a month and drank wine, ate junk food, and laughed. I went to church to sing and pray. I watched a few TV shows with Max. He started holding my hand while we sat on the couch. I don't know what he wanted. Or knew. But I didn't care. It just felt good. I went to Douglas's jazz concerts and gigs around town. I loved his energy. I visited Peter in Austin. I met his friends, ate good food, and gazed up at the star of Texas in the capital building. I slept with my husband. Sometimes I cried after he fell asleep. I went to movies with my sister. Sometimes I cried after they were over. I went shopping for hours. I spent hours returning everything.

I never heard from my inspector. I continued to look for him in the newspaper and on the local news. Not one mention. Maybe he went back to New Orleans. I couldn't blame him. I felt so good in that city. Low altitude? Lower blood pressure. No joint pain. It was as if I had shed my anxious, dry, tight skin and emerged a fresh, fearless, looser person. I was ripe and ready to burst open. But I never did.

Why did I keep thinking about James? Was it because I was bored? And he was beautiful? I didn't even know him. OK. He liked to shop at Sprouts, smelled good, owned clogs, and liked Oscar Wilde. He could have a fetish! He could love stupid TV sitcoms. He could hate open windows. He could have horrible taste in furniture! He could be a Scientologist! He could have a ferret! I knew nothing at all about him.

Too many tears! The bags under my eyes were huge. I needed a distraction. The Physics and Astronomy Reading Room was completely organized. Faye thanked me and offered to keep me on a few hours a week to help out on various administrative tasks. I said no thank you. I must move forward. No more regretting the past and fearing the future! No more thinking! Well, maybe some academic thinking. I looked into graduate schools. I loved to read. Maybe English…Creative Writing…Now there I could develop my ideal world!   Ideal sex! Like my friend Tina. She sent *The Love Crescent* off to several publishers but received rejections. Alas! At the end of the book Jesse and Pilar rode off into the sunset cooing at each other. I knew it! Hot sex helped one ignore plot holes.

But I loved mysteries. I received a passive-aggressive e-mail from the public library telling me that my books were due soon. I stacked them in the front seat and drove to Ernie Pyle Library. I parked the car on a side street, got out, and walked around to the passenger door. When I opened it, the pile of books fell out into the gutter. Oh great! I knelt down on the sidewalk and started picking them up. Someone stooped down to help me. "Thank you," I said as I stood up. There was my Inspector!

"This is my library," I said.

"I know that, Caro."

* 9 7 8 0 9 9 1 6 0 4 6 7 8 *